PICTURE
PERFECTO

PICTURE PERFECTO

By Justine, with
Devra Newberger Speregen

Illustrated by Hermine Brindak

Watson-Guptill Publications/New York

For Jordan, one truly cool dude.

Senior Editor: Julie Mazur
Editor: Cathy Hennessy
Production Manager: Katherine Happ

Text copyright © 2006 by Watson-Guptill Publications
Illustrations copyright © 2006 by Hermine Brindak

All Miss O and Friends titles, characters, and their distinctive likenesses are trademarks
of hermine design group, hdgroup, LLC© hermine design group, hdgroup, LLC 2006

First published in 2006 by Watson-Guptill Publications, a division of VNU Business Media, Inc.,
770 Broadway, New York, NY 10003
www.watsonguptill.com

Library of Congress Cataloging-in-Publication Data

Speregen, Devra Newberger.
  Miss O & friends : picture perfecto / by Justine ; with Devra Newberger Speregen ; illustrated by
Hermine Brindak.
      p. cm.
  Summary: When her father's job takes the family to Italy for the summer and fifth-grader
Justine has her best friends join her for two weeks, they find themselves in the midst of a mystery
surrounding the Palio horse race.
  ISBN-13: 978-0-8230-2949-5 (alk. paper)
  ISBN-10: 0-8230-2949-2 (alk. paper)
[1. Best friends--Fiction. 2. Friendship--Fiction. 3. Italy—Fiction. 4. Palio Festival, Siena, Italy—
Fiction. 5. Horse racing—Fiction. 6. Mystery and detective stories.] I. Brindak, Hermine, ill. II.
Title. III. Title: Miss O and friends. IV. Title: Picture perfecto.
PZ7.S7489Mip 2006
[Fic]—dc22
                          2006025107

Printed in the U.S.A.

First printing 2006

Contents

juliette   isabella   miss O   harlie   justine

Meet the group!

Welcome to Miss O and Friends!

When I, the real Juliette, was ten years old, I created the basis for Miss O and Friends. It all started when I was on the way home from a family vacation. I was bored, so I tried to think of something fun to do. The only thing that I could really do was draw. I borrowed some paper from my mom and started to draw "cool girls." I gave them to my mom and, like all mothers, she told me they were nice and put them in her purse. Little did she know that one day these drawings would turn into something much bigger.

Years later, with the help of my mom, my sister, and some friends, we started to create the Miss O girls. At first, it was just something fun to do—we'd play around on the computer creating all sorts of stuff. It wasn't until we realized that girls really liked our characters that the idea came to us to start a company. Now, thanks to girls like you, the Miss O and Friends website (www.missoandfriends.com) has become the most popular tween site ever!

The five Miss O girls are based on girls just like you and me, and they all possess important values and do things they love to do. This series of books features a story from each of the girls. Justine narrates this story—the fourth in the series. We hope you enjoy it!

Chapter 1

M . . . M . . . Moving?

Three days ago, my father got a phone call from somebody in the United States Army. My father is a general in the army (well, he's a *retired* general actually) and he has been sent to serve all over the world. Of course, my mother and I go with him wherever he's stationed, and that means we've lived in many, many different places around the world. We've moved around *a lot*. I've lived in Germany, Switzerland, France, and England, and also here in the United States, in both Texas and Colorado.

When my father retired from the army a couple of years ago, I thought all the moving around was over. And let me tell you, as fun as it is to live in faraway places and learn new languages and stuff, I am super happy that we moved back to the United States! I love my friends here in Westchester, my school, my neighborhood—everything. Westchester is perfect. So that's why, when my father got that call three days ago about a consulting job in Italy, I've been a complete mess ever since.

What will I do if he takes the job? I wondered in horror.

I mean, I'll just die! I totally don't want to move anymore. Especially now, when I've made so many close friends and I know how to get around my school. Moving would mean leaving my four VBFs (Very Best Friends) in the entire world.

Anyway, my parents told me they were going to discuss the situation on Wednesday evening (that's tonight) and make their decision by seven o'clock. Actually, my father had said, "by nineteen hundred hours," instead of "by seven o'clock," because he always talks in "army-speak." As the daughter of a general, I've had to grow up getting used to *lots* of different army phrases. (Do you know how embarrassing it is to say, "Sir, yes, sir!" to your gym teacher at school, because you're so used to hearing it on an army base? *I* do!)

Naturally, my best friends all knew about the phone call the other day (of course I told them ASAP) and about the big meeting at nineteen hundred hours tonight. They were as anxious about the meeting as I was.

I was on the phone with Juliette and Miss O. They're sisters. Juliette is a year older than Miss O, and Miss O is my age—ten, almost eleven. We're in our last year of lower division at the Sage School, which is like saying "fifth grade" at most other schools. Juliette is in first year middle division, or, sixth grade. They were doing the only thing that VBFs *could* do in this type of situation: they were talking to me on the phone to keep me from thinking about what was going on in the next room.

Our other two best friends, Harlie and Isabella, also go to the Sage School, and they're in the same grade as Miss O and me. Harlie and Isabella were not on the phone with us at the moment, but if they could have been, they would have been!

All this waiting around for the big decision made me hungry. So I popped some mini pizza bagels in the microwave. While balancing the cordless phone under my chin, I pulled the plate out of the microwave. They were hotter than I thought they'd be, and I sort of burned my fingers.

"*Ye-owch!*" I cried, nearly dropping the phone.

"What happened, Justine?" Miss O asked me as I examined my slightly singed fingers. Her name is really Olivia, but everybody calls her "Miss O" for short.

"I burned my fingers. On hot pizza bagels," I told her. "But not so bad. Just a little."

"Run them under cold water," Miss O instructed.

"Stick them in a bowl of ice," Juliette added.

"No, really guys," I said. "It's not that bad. They don't even hurt anymore. It just burned for, like, a second."

"You're lucky," Miss O told me. "I once burned my hand on a ramekin and it hurt like crazy for days!"

"What's a ramekin?" I asked her as I ran my fingers under cold water.

I could picture Miss O rolling her eyes at me on the other end of the phone. "You don't know what ramekins are?" she asked with a sigh.

"Ramekins? Uh, no. Is that even English?" I asked. "I know three languages—almost four," I told her. "But I never heard of ramekins."

Juliette piped in. "Miss O! Not everybody knows everything in the world about cooking and baking like you do!" she told her sister. "Get over yourself!"

"*Get over yourself!*" Miss O repeated, mocking her older sister's voice.

"Well how was I supposed to know Justine doesn't know what a ramekin is? It's a little dish or a tray of little molds you can bake small cakes in," she explained to me. "Kind of like muffins or cupcakes."

When my pizza bagels had cooled, I took a bite. "So when did you bake ramekins?" I asked Miss O in between chews.

"Remember a few months ago? For the school bake sale? My grandmother and I baked like four dozen chocolate lava cakes," Miss O replied.

On the other end of the phone, I heard Juliette sigh loudly. "Can we *please* talk about something else?" she asked. "This conversation is getting so lame!"

"Sure," I said. "What do you want to talk about?"

"Um, are they still in there?" Juliette asked anxiously.

From my seat at the kitchen counter, I craned my neck in order to see through the kitchen entrance and down the hall toward my father's home office. The door was still closed, and I could see light from inside the room coming through under the door.

"Yup. Still in there," I said.

"Oh, brother!" Miss O exclaimed. "This waiting is killing me!"

"Tell me about it," I said. "What am I going to do if . . . ." I couldn't even finish the sentence. The thought of it was too horrible.

"Let's not talk about *that!*" Juliette insisted. "Come on! We're trying to keep your mind *off* the big meeting. Let's talk about other things, okay?"

"Once, I baked little apple pies in a ramekin, and want to know how they came out?" Miss O said. (I could totally tell she was just trying to annoy her sister.)

And it was working.

"*Aaaarrrrrgggghhhhh!*" Juliette cried. "Not again!"

"Just kidding!" Miss O said with a chuckle.

I laughed, half-heartedly. "Okay. So what *should* we talk about?" I asked.

"How about Harlie's mom?" Miss O suggested.

I smiled as I thought about Harlie's mom. "Yeah! Great idea!" I said. Our friend Harlie's mother was about to have a baby. Well, she was still a month away, but boy was she big! She's usually a very small woman, so it's been funny to see her growing bigger and bigger each month. We were all so excited about the new baby. It was going to be a girl, and Harlie's mother had said we could all help think of some ideas for a name.

"I can see Harlie on my buddy list right now," I told the girls, pulling my laptop computer closer to where I was sitting at the counter. "Let me see if she's really online, or if there's an away message."

I clicked on Harlie's screen name and typed.

justME713: harlie? u there?

Immediately, a response came back.

harliegirl95: OMG! did u hear? what happened?
are you moving???? :o

I laughed.

justME713: no! nothing yet. still waiting.

harliegirl95: going crazy here waiting!

justME713: yeah. me2. hey — on phone
w/miss o & juliette. we're thinking
of baby names to pass the time.

harliegirl95: okay, tell!

On the phone, I told Miss O and Juliette that Harlie was online and ready to hear some of our baby name suggestions.

"Tell her mine," Miss O said. "I like Anabelle and Kiera."

"And I like Galia, Halle, and Mallory," Juliette added. "Oh, and George."

"George?" Miss O and I both asked at the same time.

"Well, more like Georgie," Juliette told us. "I think that's a cool name."

I shrugged, then began typing to Harlie.

justME713: ok, here goes: miss o likes
anabelle and kiera. juliette likes
galia, halle, and mallory. & george.
(don't ask)

harliegirl95: *george*? like *curious george*???

justME713: heh-heh. no, as in georg-ie. and i
like mikayla and alana.

harliegirl95: yeah, ok. georgie is better than
george. i'll tell mom all these
names. but i think she really likes
mei. it's chinese.

I told Miss O and Juliette about the name Mei.

"Pretty!" Miss O said.

"Yeah, cool," Juliette agreed.

> **justME713:** survey says mei is cool!
> **harliegirl95:** :)))

I was just about to type back a winking smiley to Harlie when my father's voice startled me.

"Justine," he said, clearing his throat.

My head jerked up from the computer screen. "Dad? Mom? What's up?" I asked. I could feel a lump in my throat as I spoke. The weird expressions on my parents' faces worried me.

On the other end of the phone, Miss O cried out in alarm. "Are your parents there? The big meeting is over? How do they look?"

"Are you moving?" Juliette butted in.

On the computer IM, Harlie called for me, too.

> **harliegirl95:** jus? where'd u go??? u there????
> what's going on?

Before i could speak, my father rested his hand on my shoulder.

"Justine," he said softly. "We're going to Italy."

On the other end of the line, I heard Miss O (or was it Juliette?) drop the phone.

Chapter 2
The Biggest and Best News Ever

"I gotta call you back!" I said quickly into the phone. Then I pressed the OFF button to end the call. "For real?" I asked my father with a gulp. The lump had already doubled in size. I felt like I had a golf ball stuck in my throat or something!

He nodded. "Yes," he replied.

I looked helplessly from my father to my mother, then back to my father again. "But . . . but . . . but how can you do this to me?" I asked, feeling tears well up in my eyes. Any second now and they'd be flowing like crazy. "I . . . I love it here!" I could barely get the words out. "My friends are here! I love my school—and even you said it was the best school around! I don't want to move!"

My mother stood by my side and pushed my hair away from my face. Both my mother and I have the same exact dark brown, curly hair, light brown skin, and brown eyes. Everyone always says we look so much alike. Anyway, she pushed back my hair and tucked it behind one ear—like she always does to *her* hair.

I *untucked* it.

"Mom! I don't understand!" I went on, sniffling. "I thought we all loved it here—not just me! How can we move—*again*—when everything is going so great?"

My mother took my chin in her hands. "First things first," she said gently. "Calm down."

"But . . ."

"Please, Justine. Just stop talking and calm down. There's more news."

That got me quiet.

"Huh?" I asked.

"Good news," my father added. "And we think you'll be very happy to hear it."

I seriously doubted that. There was nothing my parents could possibly tell me about moving to Italy that would make me *happy*.

I slumped into my counter stool and folded my arms across my chest.

"So as it turns out," my father began, "the job that I accepted in Italy is not a full-time job."

I stared at him. "What do you mean?" I asked.

"Well, it doesn't require that we move to Italy," my mother explained.

I sat up a little further in my seat. "But Dad said we're going to Italy," I pointed out.

Dad grinned. "We *are*," he said. "But just for the summer. The job is only for eight weeks."

I gasped with delight. "Wow! I mean, oh my gosh! Really?"

My parents both nodded. "Yes, Justine," my mother said. "Dad will just be working in Italy for the summer. In a city called Siena," she added.

"And we're both going with him?" I asked.

My mother nodded again. "Yes, honey," she said. "Actually, you and Dad are going for the first month of the summer and I'm flying out to meet you for the second month. I can't go until after the big summer fundraiser I've been working on for the community center."

I stared at my parents in disbelief. I mean, I was totally speechless! Italy . . . for the whole summer? Wow!

Then I thought about my friends—Miss O, Juliette, Harlie, and Isabella. If I went to Italy for the entire summer, I wouldn't get to hang with them at all during summer vacation. That would be a bummer. Oh, and this is just a minor thing, but if I was away all summer I wouldn't get to go to photography camp at Westchester College, which I'd been look-ing forward to all spring.

But, whatever.

I was going to Italy! *Omigod!*

And I wasn't moving after all—even *bigger omigod!*

I leapt up and hugged my parents. "Thank you so much!" I cried.

"I know you'll be sad not seeing your friends this summer," my mother said to me. "But you'll really enjoy Italy," she added. "Siena especially. It's a beautiful city, with lots to see."

"Sounds great, Mom," I told her. "But let me go IM everyone—they all think I'm moving! I have to tell them the good news!"

"Okay, honey. And maybe you can plan a pre-birthday sleepover or something with the girls before you leave."

That was a good idea, I thought. My birthday is July 13th, and since I'll be missing celebrating it with my friends, it would be fun to do something before I left for Italy. Maybe after the last day of school next week, I thought.

I returned to the laptop and touched the mouse to activate the screen. I laughed when I noticed four open IMs blinking and waiting for me. They looked like this:

> **gOalgirl:** OMGOMGOMG, justine! what's going
> on? you cant be moving!!!!!!
>
> **jujuBEE:** r u really moving? this stinx!
>
> **IzzyBella:** i just heard! im freaking out! call me!
>
> **harliegirl95:** HOLY MOLEY! this is the worst
> newz ever!

I groaned. It was going to take forever to get back to them all. So I decided to open a chat room .

> **justME713:** hey — you all here?

gOalgirl: yes! im freaking out here, justine!

jujuBEE: i'm here 2 — what's going on?

IzzyBella: jus — are you really moving?

harliegirl95: we're all here, justine. what's the story?

justME713: ok — here's the deal: i'm **not** moving!!!! :))))))))

gOalgirl: but your father said ur going 2 italy???

justME713: that's cuz i am going 2 italy!

harliegirl95: huh?

IzzyBella: justine!!!!!!!!

justME713: here's the 411: my father is taking that job. but it's not a forever job! just 4 the summer! so i'm going to italy 4 the summer!

jujuBEE: so ur not moving?

justME713: not moving! :)

harliegirls956: yipee!

gOalgirl: that's awesome! omg, i'm so happy! :))))))))))))))))))))))))))))))

IzzyBella: hooray!

We chatted for a little while longer, making plans for the big pre-birthday sleepover. The girls were bummed that I wouldn't be around for the summer, but they were way happy to hear I wasn't moving after all!

After a few more IMs, I logged out of the chat to do some research. Lucky for me, I'm pretty good at surfing the Web, and I found a lot of interesting facts about Siena. For instance, it's located in the Tuscany region of Italy. And it's pretty close to Pisa, where the famous Leaning Tower of Pisa is. I've always wanted to see that!

I decided I would bring both my cameras to Italy this summer. You see, I'm very into photography. I want to be a photojournalist when I grow up. Maybe work for an international fashion magazine. (That is my dream job!) Anyway, I have two cameras—one is a digital camera that I use for taking "fun" pictures: of my friends, at parties, stuff like that.

My other camera was a gift from my parents last year for my tenth birthday. It's an expensive, professional 35-millimeter camera. It's not just a "point and shoot" camera like my digital. It's much harder to use! It took me a whole month to learn how to hold it properly and to adjust the focus and shutter speeds. But it takes the most amazing photographs. I use this camera for special photos—of scenery, on vacations, and for portraits.

Thinking about my 35-millimeter, I have to admit I felt pretty bad about not getting to go to that photography camp this summer. Especially because I was supposed to learn how to develop my own photographs in a real darkroom.

Oh, well! Maybe next summer!

This summer, I was getting the chance of a lifetime! A whole summer exploring Italy!

The following afternoon, I sat at the kitchen counter working on an "end of the year" assignment that my teacher, Mrs. Spanos, had given the class. We really don't get a lot of work during the last two weeks of school (it's all about playing games and class parties!), but Mrs. Spanos says she doesn't want our minds to go to waste over the summer just because there is no school. So at the end of the school year every year, she gives her class an assignment: to come up with a list of five interesting things we plan to do over the summer vacation. Then we're supposed to send her a letter once we accomplished each thing, describing what it was like. It wasn't homework or anything, and we wouldn't be graded on it, but it sounded like fun so I was psyched to do it. And anyway, I had way more than five interesting things I'd be doing this summer, so this assignment was going to be a cinch!

I was just adding "Photograph the Leaning Tower of Pisa in Italy" to my list, when I heard the doorbell ring.

"I got it!" I called through the house. I pulled open the front door, and to my surprise, there stood Miss O and Juliette . . . and their parents!

"Uh, hey! What's up?" I asked in confusion. "What's going on? What are you guys doing here?"

Both Miss O and Juliette seemed as bewildered as me.

Juliette made a face and shrugged. "We're not really sure," she said. "Our parents just said, 'Get in the car, we have a stop to make,' so we did."

"Mom?" Miss O asked her mother. "So, what are we doing at Justine's house?"

Before Miss O's mother could answer, two more cars pulled up on my driveway.

"Is that Isabella's car?" I asked. "And . . . and . . . Harlie's father's car? What on earth is going on?"

Miss O's parents didn't answer me. They just stepped inside the house and left us kids standing in the doorway—more confused than ever.

"What are you doing here?" I called out to Isabella as she and her parents walked up my driveway.

Isabella shrugged. "I'm not sure," she replied.

"Hey, Justine! Hi, guys!" Harlie called as she stepped out of her father's car. Her father walked around to the passenger's side and helped her mother out of the car. Wow, I thought to myself. Harlie's mom had gotten even bigger since last week!

I turned into the house and called out to my parents. "Mom? Dad?" My voice rang through the hallway. "What's going on? Why is everybody here?"

Finally, my parents appeared in the foyer. "Everyone here?" my mother asked.

My friends' parents all nodded.

This was so *weird!*

"Can someone please tell us what's going on?" I asked again. "Why are all my best friends here . . . on a school night?"

My father grinned mysteriously. "Justine," he said. "And Olivia, Juliette, Harlie and Isabella," he added, "we have some important news for you."

My stomach tightened when he said that. I got instantly nervous. Did this important news have anything to do with me going to Italy? I wondered. Had the situation changed again? And was this my parents' way of telling me I was really moving???

"Dad, what's going on? You're scaring me," I said.

My father smiled. "The news is not scary, Justine," he said. "It's great news, as a matter of fact."

My friends and I all exchanged confused looks.

"What is it?" Miss O asked.

"Yeah, what's the news?" Harlie wanted to know.

"Please, tell us!" Juliette added. "The suspense is killing us!"

My mother laughed. So did a few of the other adults. "Well," she said, "you all know how Justine is going to Italy this summer, right?"

The girls all nodded.

"And you're all going to miss her terribly, right?" she asked.

The girls nodded harder and faster.

"I know! So we're all getting webcams to hook up to our computers!" Harlie guessed. "So we can see her and talk to her whenever we want!"

Harlie's mother held her big fat belly and laughed. "Oh, Harlie!" she said.

Harlie grinned.

"Well, no, we're going to do one better than that," my father said.

We all stared at him in suspense.

"How about . . . if you all came to Italy with us?" he asked. Just like that.

Nobody said a word for at least a full minute. Finally, I spoke.

"Dad, what are you talking about?" I asked.

"It's just like your father said," Miss O's father explained. "What would you all think if we agreed to let you girls go to Italy with Justine and her father for two whole weeks this summer?"

My eyes widened in shock. "You mean . . . all of us?" I asked.

My mother nodded. "Well, not us parents," she explained. "Just you girls. How about it?" she asked my friends. "Would you all like to go with Justine to Italy?"

I gazed at my friends' excited faces. In our foyer it was dead quiet at first, then everyone started talking at once.

"Really, Dad?" Isabella asked.

"Both of us?" Juliette asked her father.

"For two whole weeks?" Harlie asked her parents.

My father held up his hand. (I was secretly glad he wasn't wearing his whistle this evening, because that's how he usually got people's attention. And that would have been truly embarrassing.)

"Whoa!" he said. "Hang on! We'll answer everybody's questions . . . but not all at once!"

My mother continued. "We moms and dads got to talking last night, and we all agreed it would be a wonderful experience for you girls to go to Italy together. We've already arranged for a tour guide and a chaperone for you for when Justine's father has to work. And you can all stay in the apartment the military is providing for Justine's father. It's right in the center of town, and it has three very large bedrooms."

"It's our 'moving up' gift to you all," Isabella's mother added. "For graduating from lower division. And for doing so well in school this past year."

"But what about me?" Juliette asked. "I graduated from lower division *last year*!"

"Okay, then you can't go," her father joked.

"Hey!" Justine wailed, even though I knew that she knew he was just kidding.

"Your grades this year were terrific, too, Juliette," her mother said. "We're very proud of you. Of all of you," she added. "So this is our way of saying, 'Way to go!'"

"And, 'Happy moving up!'" my father chimed in.

As it slowly began to sink in that this was no joke—that we were all going to Italy together for two entire weeks—the five of us became too stunned to speak. Too shocked to form words and put them into sentences. Instead, we just hugged each other and jumped up and down, screeching with excitement.

"Moving up" instead of "Moving away."

Boy, was I happy!

But it was Harlie who finally found just the right words.

"*Mamma mia!*" she cried. "We're going to Italy!"

Chapter 3

Chillin' on the Piazza!

I was pretty tired from the long flight to Rome (we left at 6 A.M. in the morning!) and then the long drive from the airport to Siena, but the most tiring part about my first day in Italy was lugging my big, fat suitcase and super-heavy backpack up four flights of stairs to the *residenza* (hotel apartment) we were renting! The apartment was on the Via Montanini (Montanini Street), a side street that led into the city square, which was called a *"piazza."* As I watched my father use the key to open the door, I'm telling you, I was panting like a puppy.

But when we stepped inside the residenza, I completely forgot how tired I was.

Oh my gosh! It was *amazing!*

"Holy . . . cannoli!" Harlie exclaimed as we entered what I guessed was the living room.

We all looked at her.

"What?" she asked with a grin. "That's my new expression for Italy: Holy cannoli! Cannolis are my favorite Italian pastries."

We all laughed. But Harlie was right: Holy cannoli, this was the most awesome apartment ever!

First of all, the living room was huge, with not two, but *three* comfy couches! And it was so spacious, you could fit, like, all of Mrs. Spanos' class in it for a social studies lesson. Plus, all the windows were huge— they started about a foot from the floor and went all the way up to the high ceiling!

"Darn!" Harlie muttered as we wandered through the rooms.

"What's the matter, Harlie?" Isabella asked.

"I should have brought my Wheelys!" Harlie said. "These ceramic tile floors and wide open spaces are perfect for wheelying!" Ever since last Chinese New Year, when Harlie's parents bought her new Wheely sneakers (sneakers with wheels), she's been obsessed.

I laughed, picturing Harlie wheelying all over Siena. Then I moved closer to the windows to check out the view. "Wow!" I cried. "We have a terrace!"

"A *terrazzo*," my father corrected me. "That's Italian for terrace."

"Whatever it's called, it's so cool!" I replied. "Come check it out!"

I pulled open the double doors and stepped onto the terrazzo, with my friends following me close behind. Once outside, I let out a gasp.

"Boy! It's beautiful!" I cried.

"*Bella!*" Isabella said. "That means 'beautiful.' The stewardess on the plane told me that. We should start speaking a little Italian," she added.

"I promised my parents I would try anyway. It's a good idea to keep the brain busy during summer vacation, my mother always says."

"That's exactly what Mrs. Spanos says!" I told her. "Okay," I added. "It's a deal. Let's speak Italian whenever we can," I said to my friends.

"*Sì!*" Miss O said. "That means 'Yes!'"

"*Bene,*" Juliette added. "That means 'good'!"

"Spaghetti!" Harlie chimed in.

We all cracked up.

"Well that's the only Italian I know!" she insisted. "That . . . and cannoli."

"You probably know much more than that," I told her, "but you just don't realize it. Like, 'thank you', for instance. How do you think you say that in Italian?"

Harlie shrugged.

"I know!" Isabella announced. "It's '*grazie!*' Italian is a lot like Spanish, and in Spanish, 'thank you' is '*gracias.*'"

"Right!" I said. But I knew Isabella would know that. Italian *is* a lot like Spanish, and Isabella speaks Spanish fluently because she's from South America. Peru, actually. And she speaks Spanish at home with her mother and stepfather, who is from Argentina. "Anyway," I went on, "you'll be surprised to see how many Italian words you know."

"So that's the Piazza del Campo," my father pointed out to us as we stood on the terrazzo, overlooking the city square below. There were shops and cafés lined up all around the piazza, and a beautiful fountain. There was a lot of activity taking place down below as we looked down.

"Hey, they're playing soccer on the piazza!" Miss O told us.

I nodded. Miss O is a die-hard soccer fan. She's also a great soccer player. I go to all of her games, and she scores a goal almost every time! Next season, she says, she's trying out for the traveling team. Me? I'm not much up for sports. I like to do yoga and I like to play tennis, but I don't care much for team sports.

"Let's unpack," Juliette said suddenly. "Then maybe we can go for a walk before it gets dark?"

We all looked up at my father to see what he thought about Juliette's idea.

"Sure!" he said. "I'm anxious to have a look around, too. Not to mention sip a little cappuccino."

"Cappuccino!" Harlie cried. "I know what that is! I guess I *do* know a lot of Italian!"

We all laughed because everyone knows what cappuccino is. Especially Harlie—who is a huge Starbucks freak! She likes decaf mocha lattes so much, she and her mother go to Starbucks nearly every day. They're making a list of all the Starbucks coffee shops they've been to and trying to visit every Starbucks in Manhattan.

The bedroom we all were sharing was even larger than my parents' master bedroom back at home in Westchester. It was humongous! It had two big beds in it and a sleeper sofa, so we could all bunk together. Miss O and I shared one bed, Juliette and Isabella shared the other bed, and Harlie slept on the sleeper sofa. Harlie wasn't upset that nobody wanted to share with her—it was common knowledge from years of sleepovers that Harlie "kicked" a lot when she slept.

It took me all of about three minutes to unpack! I was so anxious to get out and explore, I just stuffed my clothes into two dresser drawers. Unlike Juliette, who had to examine each piece of clothing she brought with her as she removed it from her suitcase. A suitcase, I should mention, that was larger than mine . . . and I was staying for the whole summer!

"Do you think I'll get to wear this skirt?" she asked us, holding up a pretty peasant skirt that had a few jingly things attached to the drawstrings.

I shrugged. "I don't know. Maybe if we go somewhere fancy shmancy?"

"Can't we finish unpacking later?" Miss O asked. "I want to see the piazza."

"Me, too," Harlie added.

Juliette hung her peasant skirt neatly on a hanger in the closet, then closed her suitcase. "Sure," she said. "I can finish unpacking later."

"How many outfits did you actually bring?" I asked her.

"A lot," Juliette replied. "It was so hard to choose!" she added. "I didn't know what I would need or how hot or cold it would be. So I took along something for every type of weather! I have skirts, shorts, skorts, jeans, tees, tanks . . . "

Miss O sighed loudly and fell onto one of the beds. "Oh, great! You just had to ask!" she joked.

Luckily, my father called for us just then. "Ready, girls?" he asked.

"Yes! We're coming!" I replied.

I pulled a red silk scarf from my backpack and I tied it around my hair. I had seen a model wearing a scarf just like it in a magazine last week and I thought it had looked really cool. Very European and hip! It was exactly how I wanted to look while in Italy.

I grabbed my camera and we all headed out the door and down to the Piazza del Campo. We were ready for our first day in Italy!

Miss O just couldn't help herself. She begged us to stop so she could kick the soccer ball around with the Italian boys. We watched as she did her best to keep up with them.

"They are way too good!" she said breathlessly as she wiped her forehead with her arm. "They kept doing all these tricks and stuff. I wish I could play soccer like that!"

We walked around the piazza for a little while longer, but many of the shops were closed for the day. So we headed back to the flat. As we approached the building, I gazed up at the *terrazzi* and counted up four flights. "That's our terrazzo!" I told the girls.

"You're right!" Juliette said. "We have the best terrazzo in all of Siena!" she decided. "We can hang out up there and see everything going on down here."

"Hey! Check it out!" Harlie interrupted. "There's an outdoor café right downstairs in our building! That is so cool!"

"Let's go see," Miss O suggested.

"Can we, Dad?" I asked.

"Absolutely," he replied. "I'm just about ready for my cappuccino!"

"Maybe they have ice cream," Isabella said.

"Mmmmm, ice cream right downstairs from our hotel?" Harlie muttered. "Italy just keeps getting better and better!"

We sat down in the outdoor part of the café so we could people-watch as we ate. A waitress came by to take our order and shook her head when Harlie ordered ice cream.

"No ice cream!" she said in English with a lovely Italian accent.

We all frowned.

"Oh, phooey!" Harlie said.

"No!" the waitress said again. "You don't understand. We don't have ice cream. In Italy we have gelato!"

We all looked at each other.

"You will like gelato!" the waitress promised. "It is better than the ice cream!"

I was in Italy, and I was up for trying the gelato. So were the other girls.

P.S., the gelato was excellent! I liked it even better than ice cream! It was lighter and fluffier. I ordered strawberry, which came with little pieces of strawberries in it.

"Do they make gelato in Westchester?" Isabella asked as she ate her apple gelato.

We all looked at my father.

He shrugged. "I'm not sure," he said.

"We'll have to check that out when we get home," I said.

"Yeah," Harlie agreed. "Because I just found my new favorite food!" She smiled as she swallowed a spoonful of blueberry gelato.

I gazed around the café, which was decorated with bright colored flags and posters of Italy and Siena. It was so pretty! It reminded me of the café my mother and I went to every morning for breakfast when we lived in Paris.

Mmmmm . . . it even *smelled* like that café!

I took in another sniff, then I scooped up some more strawberry gelato. I was so happy! We hadn't even been in Siena for a whole day, yet I was already having the time of my life. I was with my dad, my very best buds, chilling in the center of an Italian city . . . eating gelato.

What could be bad?

I pulled out my camera and started taking pictures. It was getting dark, so I was glad I'd taken along my flash. I focused, set the shutter speed on low, and snapped away at whatever I could. Most of the pictures were of the girls—with different-colored gelato all over their mouths! As I took the pictures, I knew we would always look at them and laugh.

I got up from our table to look for something else to photograph. As I stood inside the café, I aimed my camera outside for a picture. When I snapped, the flash went off and startled a pretty, young Italian woman who was on her way out of the café. So much so, that she dropped her box of pastries!

"Oh! I'm so sorry!" I cried. "I'm really, really—" I stopped myself in mid-sentence. I mean, this was Italy, I reminded myself, and I was apologizing in English. This woman probably had no idea what I was saying!

"I'm really sorry!" I said again, bending down to pick up the pastry box.

To my surprise the woman replied, "You say, '*mi scusi.*' "It means, 'I'm sorry.'"

"Oh! Okay," I replied. "Then, mi scusi. . . a lot!" I added. (I know it sounded stupid, but it was the best I could do.)

The woman laughed. To my relief, she seemed perfectly pleasant and not angry at all. I handed her the pastry box.

Then she surprised me again. "You are Justine, no?" she asked.

Chapter 4
Not Just Any ol' Horse Race!

I stood in the café with my jaw hanging open.

How in the world did she know my name?

"Um, yes," I said cautiously. "I'm Justine. But how did you—"

The woman held out the box of cannolis that she had just picked up from the floor. "Okay, Justine! These are for you!" she announced. "I hope they are not, how do you say, broke?"

"Oh, er, broken?" I asked.

"Yes! I hope they are not broken! They are special *paste* from Siena." She pushed her long, dark black hair behind her shoulders and smiled, showing two rows of the whitest teeth I had ever seen.

"Ew. Paste?" I asked.

"*Sì! Paste. Il dolci* . . . desserts. Like cannoli, biscotti . . . "

"Oh! You mean pastries!" I exclaimed, feeling very proud of myself for figuring it out.

"*Sì!* Yes! Pastries," she repeated slowly. "They are for you!"

"Oh! Well, uh, thank you," I replied. "But, how come you're giving me pastries? And how do you know me?"

The woman laughed, and her dark eyes sparkled. "Ah, *scusi!* Excuse me! I am sorry I did not tell you before. *Mi chiamo* Gia Reganato. That is how you say, 'My name is,' in Italian. My name is Gia Reganato. I am your guide."

Our guide?

Oh, right! Our tour guide and chaperone!

"Duh!" I said. "Of course! Who else would know my name in Italy?" I said with a laugh.

"Duh?" Gia asked.

I felt my face turn red. "Never mind," I told her. "It's just a word kids say to mean, 'no kidding'! It's sarcastic. You know, like that it's silly I couldn't figure out who you were on my own."

Gia smiled and gazed around the café. "So *Benvenuto!* Welcome to Italy! Where is your *padre?*" she asked. "Your father? And your friends?"

"They are sitting outside eating gelato," I told her. "Come with me. I'll introduce you!"

When we reached the table, I caught Harlie eating my gelato.

She licked her lips. "Uh, I thought you were finished," she said sheepishly.

I laughed. "It's okay," I told her. "I was. Anyway, guys, this is Gia! She is our guide—I just met her inside the café. Isn't that a coincidence? I made her drop the paste in the café."

The girls looked at me strangely.

"'Le paste' means pastries," I explained. "Gia came by the café to get some 'Welcome to Italy' pastries for us. She was on her way up to the hotel to meet us when my flash startled her and made her drop the box."

"Oh, no! Did they break?" Harlie asked. She looked worried.

"I don't think so," I told her. Harlie was so protective when it came to food. "Anyway, Gia, this is my father."

Gia and my dad shook hands.

"And these are my buds," I explained. "My friends. Miss O, that's short for Olivia; Juliette, but sometimes we call her Juje; Isabella, who also answers to Izzy; and that's Harlie with the gelato mustache."

The girls all giggled. Mainly because Harlie's mustache was blue, and she looked ridiculous.

"You like our gelato?" Gia asked Harlie.

"Yes!" Harlie replied enthusiastically. "Very much! How do you say 'very much' in Italian?"

"*Molto*," Gia told her.

"I like gelato molto!" Harlie replied.

"Wow, you can translate everything for us," Juliette said. "We'll know how to speak Italian by the time we leave!"

Gia laughed. "Well, I don't know about that," she said. "But I'll teach you all the words you want to know. Just ask."

"I have one," I said. "How do you say 'camera'?" I thought that might be useful for me to know.

"*Macchina fotografica*," she said.

"Wow! All that for 'camera'?" I said. Maybe I'd just stick to "camera."

Miss O giggled. "What about 'goodbye'?" she asked. "How do you say, 'goodbye'?"

"Well, with friends you can simply say "*ciao*", Gia explained.

"Oh! I knew that!" I told them all. "Mrs. Spanos taught us that in school!"

Isabella pointed to a poster of horses, hanging on the café wall. "Oh! How do you say 'horse'?" she asked. I don't know if I mentioned it before, but Isabella is a horse *freak*. She loves everything about horses.

Gia's eyes lit up. "Horse is *cavallo*!" she said excitedly. "Do you like horses?" she asked.

Isabella's eyes widened. "Yes! I love horses," she said. "I ride at home all the time," she went on. "I learned when I was little."

"My papà," Gia told us, "he raises race horses. He is a very famous man in Siena. Many of his horses have gone on to win the Palio."

"The what?" I asked her.

Gia's big brown eyes widened. "You mean," she asked slowly, "you don't know about the Palio?"

We all looked at each other and shook our heads. "Isabella, do you know?" I asked.

Isabella made a face. "Nope. Never heard of it," she replied.

"So, what is the Palio?" Miss O asked.

Gia shook her head in disbelief. As if it were a crime to never have heard of the Palio! That's when she pulled an empty chair away from another table over to our table and sat down.

"I must tell you about the Palio!" she said firmly. "You cannot come to Siena in the summertime and not know about the Palio!"

Sensing the seriousness in her voice, I grabbed an empty chair, too, and sat in between my father and Miss O. We all leaned in closer to listen to Gia.

"Every summer, in July, on the second of July, we have the Palio in Siena. For hundreds of years we have had this!"

"But what is it, exactly?" Miss O asked.

"The Palio is a horse race!" Gia stated.

"A horse race?" Isabella asked.

Gia startled us by throwing up her hands. "Well, not just a horse race!" she exclaimed. "It is the Palio! The most important horse race in all of *Italia!* Maybe, in all of the world!"

"Wow," Harlie said. "And it's right here in Siena? Cool! We'll be here on July second, right?" she asked my father.

He nodded. "Yes," he replied. "July second is just six days from today."

I smiled. "Gia, we will be here to see the Palio!" I told her. "Can we come? How do we get tickets?"

Gia laughed. "You do not need tickets to come to the Palio!" she said. "Everybody in Siena comes to the Palio!"

"Are we near the racetrack?" Juliette asked.

Gia laughed again, as if Juliette's question was the funniest thing she had ever heard. "Sì! Sì! You are very near to the race track!" she replied. She got up from her chair and held out her arms, facing the Piazza del Campo. "Here!" she told us. "In the Piazza del Campo! *This* is the race-track!"

"You're kidding!" I said in amazement. "You mean the horses race around the piazza?"

Gia nodded. "Sì, Justine. There are ten horses that race in the Palio," she explained. "The horses are chosen three days before the race, from seventeen neighborhoods in Siena. Our neighborhoods are called *contrade*. Each *contrada* races a horse. They search all over the world for the best *fantini*."

"Fantini?" I asked. "What's a fantini?"

"A *fantino* is a jockey,'" Gia explained.

"A jockey is the person who rides the horse during a race," Isabella pointed out. "Like Elliott, the man who owns the stables I ride at back at home. He used to be a famous jockey in America. He once raced in the Kentucky Derby!"

Gia nodded. "Yes, that is a fantino," she said. "Sometimes, a contrada will get a jockey from America, too. Whoever is the best! The Palio is the most important event in Siena all year. We think about the Palio all year long," she added. "Winning the Palio—the special banner—is the highest honor in all of Siena!"

"Oooh! I really want to see the Palio!" Isabella exclaimed.

"You cannot miss it," Gia assured us. "In six days, all of Siena will be at your doorstep. Every single person! Nobody misses the Palio. And you are lucky to have the best seats in the country! Right on your terrazzo!"

I clasped my hands together in excitement. I couldn't even imagine what that would be like, watching the Palio from our terrazzo. Did all of Siena really come to watch, like Gia said? How many people would that be? I wondered.

"And there's much more to the Palio," Gia added. "There are many parties and parades and dinners with dancing and singing and cheering. This is indeed the best time to come to Siena!"

The girls and I exchanged excited looks. How cool!

"Gia, does your father have a horse in the race this summer?"

"Of course!" Gia exclaimed. "He has been training one special horse all year long! Our beautiful horse, Scroscio. I know she will win the Palio this year!"

"Scroscio?" I asked. "What does that name mean?"

"It is the sound of applause," Gia explained. "And that is what we will hear when Scroscio crosses the finish line next week!"

"Wow, this is so exciting!" Isabella gushed. "Justine, can you believe we came to Siena just in time for this? We are so, so lucky!"

"*Gia!*" a voice suddenly called out.

We all spun around to see who had called our new friend. Across the street, on the opposite corner from the café, stood a young boy in a soccer uniform.

"That is my brother, Marco," Gia told us. She called out to him, something in Italian that we couldn't understand. But the weird thing was, from the tone of their voices I got the feeling they were arguing. And that Marco didn't want to come over and meet us!

"*Scusa,*" Gia said softly. "Excuse me." Then she walked across the street to talk to her brother. When she returned a few minutes later, Marco was with her, walking behind her more than a little reluctantly.

"Oh my gosh! He is so cute!" Juliette whispered to me.

When Gia introduced him to us, I could see why Juliette was already crushing. Marco *was* cute. He had dark curly hair and big, dark eyes like his sister.

"This is Marco. My brother," Gia said. "He is fourteen years old."

We all smiled and said hello.

Marco smiled back and Juliette kicked me under the table.

"*Molto lieto.* Nice to meet you," he said to us. Then he turned back to his sister. "*Andiamo!* Let's go!" he said anxiously.

We all exchanged confused looks. Boy, how rude!

Gia, I could tell, felt bad. She was obviously embarrassed by her brother's behavior. "I must go to take Marco home now," she said unhappily. "He has just finished playing soccer. I am very sorry. But we will come early for you tomorrow. Marco will come sightseeing with us, too, if that is okay?"

I opened my mouth to say, "Sure, that's okay," but Juliette beat me to it!

"Oh, yes! He can come with us! Sure! Um, right?" she added, turning to ask my father if it were indeed okay.

My father smiled. "Of course. Marco is welcome to join us," he said. "Actually, I won't be joining you sightseeing tomorrow," he added. "I have work to do. But I'm sure you girls will have a wonderful day with Gia and Marco."

"*Grazie mille*," Gia said. "Thank you very much. Okay! We will see you tomorrow!"

"Okay, Gia," I said, suddenly finding myself having to yawn. I realized I was seriously tired. I didn't know what time it was exactly, but because of the seven-hour time difference between Italy and New York, and the crazy jet lag from the flight, I suddenly felt as though I could sleep for two days straight! "We'll be ready, Gia," I promised, stifling a second yawn.

Marco said goodbye, too. "I am very sorry not to sit with you longer," he apologized. "But my sister knows I do not ever want to come to this café! It is *veleno*! Poison!"

I watched as Marco's face got redder. Then he took a deep breath and calmed down.

"So, good night, girls. *Arrivederci!*"

He walked away and we all exchanged very confused looks.

"Did Marco just call this café . . . 'poison'?" Harlie asked.

I nodded and stared at my friends in disbelief.

"Yes. I think he did," I replied.

Chapter 5
Tower vs. Tortoise

"That was so weird!" Juliette said as we walked upstairs to our residenza.

"Tell me about it!" I agreed. I turned to my father, who was a few steps behind me. "Dad, why do you think Marco said that about the café?" I asked.

"I don't know, Justine," he said. "It was strange. Maybe he had some bad biscotti there once?" Dad offered.

I laughed, but honestly, I had the feeling Marco's disgust with the café was nothing to joke about. You had to see his face when he spoke about the café! It was as if he hated the place with a passion!

We reached the residenza, and I couldn't stop yawning —that's how sleepy I was. I noticed Miss O and Isabella were rubbing their eyes, too, and Harlie looked like she was already sleeping . . . as she walked!

"I think you girls ought to go to bed," my father said once we were inside. "You have an early start tomorrow."

"Okay, Dad," I said. Nobody protested. We were all beat.

We changed into pajamas and climbed into our beds. Juliette pulled apart the curtains so we could see the view of the tops of the buildings along the piazza. It was a cool idea, but I think I fell asleep before she got the curtains completely open! The last thing I heard was Miss O's voice.

"Maybe tomorrow we can ask Gia why her brother hates the café so much," she said with a yawn.

We all mumbled a reply, then drifted off to sleep on our first night in Italy.

I woke up first the next morning, and, luckily, I felt great! Full of energy! I woke the others and headed into the bathroom to wash up. Then I pulled on my favorite peasant skirt, a chocolate brown tank top, and my favorite walking sandals. I found another silk scarf in my bag and I tied it around my hair again. I was really digging this "look"! I brushed my teeth, then my hair, then headed into the kitchen.

My father was already busy preparing breakfast for us when we walked into the kitchen. "Whatcha making, Dad?" I asked. He looked so funny—wearing a flowered apron—I almost laughed out loud.

"It smells great in here!" Harlie exclaimed, stepping into the kitchen right behind me.

"I'm making Italian pancakes!" my father replied. "Come sit down and try some!"

We all took seats around the kitchen table as my father began doling out the Italian pancakes. I stared at my pancakes in confusion. They looked like your normal, everyday pancakes.

"Dad, what's the difference between Italian pancakes and regular pancakes?" I asked.

Dad grinned. "Nothing, honey," he replied.

My friends and I all exchanged looks.

"Then why are these called Italian pancakes?" Isabella asked.

"Well, because I made them in Italy!" my father answered.

"Ha! Good one!" Harlie said, digging into her Italian pancakes. "Justine! Pass the Italian orange juice, please!" she cried.

I laughed and gave her the bottle of juice.

"And I'll have a glass of Italian milk, please!" Juliette requested.

"*Mmmmm!* These Italian pancakes are so much better than Westchester pancakes!" Miss O said as she munched. "Do you think it's because they are made with Italian eggs?"

"No!" I told her. "It's because you are eating them on an Italian plate!"

We joked about the Italian silverware, the Italian fruit, and the Italian table and chairs for the next ten minutes or so as we ate. We were still laughing when Gia arrived.

"*Buon giorno!*" Gia announced as she entered the kitchen. "That means, 'good morning'!" She looked so pretty, in a white tank top and a long, white skirt. Her black hair hung down to the middle of her back, and it was so shiny! I sometimes wished my own kinky, curly hair was as straight and shiny as that!

"Good morning!" Gia repeated in English. "You are all so happy this morning?"

"Yes! That's because we are eating authentic Italian pancakes!" Harlie told her excitedly.

We all laughed because Gia looked so confused.

"Italian pancakes?" she asked.

"It's an inside joke," I explained to her. "Dad made it up this morning. And it's not even that funny!" I added with a smile to my father. "We're all just being silly."

"Oh! Like 'duh'?" Gia asked.

My jaw fell open. I couldn't believe she'd remembered that from yesterday!

"Well, not exactly," I said.

"You taught Gia the word 'duh'?" Miss O asked.

I made a face. "Well, not intentionally," I said. "I just sort of used it and she asked me what it meant. It's a hard word to explain, you know! A lot harder than, say, ramekins!"

"Ram-e-kins?" Gia asked slowly. "What is this ramekins?"

"Oh, no! Not again!" Juliette cried, putting her head down on the table.

Dad interrupted us as he pulled off his flowery apron and stuffed his Blackberry and laptop into his briefcase. "Sorry, everyone, but it's time for me to go," he said.

I frowned. "I wish you could come with us today, Dad," I said.

"Me, too, sweetie. But I've got people to meet and papers to prepare," he replied. "And I'd like to be able to take time off for the Palio," he added, "especially after Gia said it was really something not to miss."

"Sì! Yes!" Gia said. "You cannot be in Siena this time of year and miss the Palio. It is not possible."

Dad leaned over to kiss my head. As he did, he placed something on the table in front of me. It was a cell phone!

"Dad!" I cried. "Is this for me?"

Dad grinned and nodded. "Yes," he said. "I thought you should have a cell phone while we are in Italy this summer. It will make me feel better knowing you girls are just a phone call away."

I was ecstatic! My own cell—for the whole summer! I could tell the girls were psyched for me, too. Other than Juliette, none of us has our own cells.

"Cool! Thanks, Dad!"

"You're welcome. Now, promise me you'll have a *favoloso* day!" he told us.

Gia laughed. "Your Italian is *molto bene*." she told my father. "Very good!"

"*Grazie!*" Dad replied. Then, with a wink to us all, he walked out the door.

"We all want to try to speak in Italian, too," I told Gia after he left. "We're going to try to use a couple of new words each day. Then, by the time we get home, we will know a lot of Italian."

"*Eccellente!*" Gia replied. "That means—"

"Excellent!" we all chimed in.

Gia laughed. "Sì! Well, I suppose that was an easy one!"

When we'd finished eating, we headed downstairs to Gia's car. Actually, it was not a car, but a small, white minivan. Gia said my father had rented it for us to tour in. She was glad because her own car is a sports car with room for only two.

"Today," Gia told us as we piled into the van, "we will go to my home, the Reganato estate. I wish for you to meet my *padre*. And, of course, to meet Scroscio!"

"Cool!" we all agreed. We were all very anxious to meet the horse Gia said will win the Palio!

"I'm so excited!" Isabella announced. "Do you think your father will let us pet Scroscio?" she asked.

"Absolutely!" she said as she pulled away from the *residenza*. "You can groom her, too. But no riding her . . . not until after the Palio!"

As we headed toward Gia's family estate—which she said was just a few kilometers away—I felt Miss O kick my leg.

"Ow—" I started to protest, but then I realized she was giving me a weird look. "*What?*" I whispered to her. "*Why did you just kick me like that?*"

"*Sorry!*" Miss O whispered back. "*But I wanted to remind you we were going to ask Gia about Marco and what he said about the café!*"

Right! I'd completely forgotten!

I nodded to Miss O, then I leaned forward to speak to Gia.

"Gia? Can I ask you something?"

"Sì! What is it, Justine?"

"Okay," I began. "Well, last night, when you left to take Marco home, you walked away and Marco said something to us that was really weird."

"Sì?"

"He said he hates the café," I told her. "That he doesn't go there because it is poison. What did he mean?"

Gia shook her head as she drove. "It is all because of the Palio," she explained.

"Huh? I don't get it," I replied.

"You see, the café below your *residenza*, it is owned by a family from a different *contrada*."

I made a face. "Contrada?" I asked.

"That's another neighborhood, remember?" Isabella asked. "Gia told us yesterday that there are seventeen different neighborhoods in Siena that try to enter a horse to race in the Palio."

"Sì, Isabella. You are right," Gia said. "And the café, it is owned by a family from the *contrada della Tartuca*."

"*Tartuca?*" Juliette asked. "What's that mean?"

"It is, how do you say in English, a little slow crawler?" Gia asked.

We all exchanged looks.

"A little slow crawler?" I repeated.

"Sì, a little animal. He crawls and lives in a shell?"

"A turtle?" Harlie asked.

"Sì!" Gia cried. "But it's more like a tortoise! Tartuca!"

"That's a weird name for a neighborhood," Miss O commented.

"It is part of our history," Gia explained. "Each neighborhood was originally represented by an animal. Many, many years ago. The Palio is very different now, from when it began in the sixteen-hundreds. But the contrade still keep their names. Our contrada is called *Torre*. Like the *Torre del Mangia*."

"Huh? What is that?" I asked.

"The Torre del Mangia!" Gia exclaimed. "Torre! Look out the window, you will see a Torre. The Torre del Mangia."

We all leaned toward the closest windows and gazed outside the van. In the distance, we could see the buildings from the Piazza del Campo.

"Torre, torre, torre," Miss O mumbled as she peered across the landscape towards the piazza we'd left a little while ago. "I see buildings and a tower," she said.

"Sì! Yes! A tower! Torre!" she said excitedly.

"Oh! Torre means tower!" Miss O said proudly. I guessed it!"

"This is the name of our *contrada*," Gia repeated. "Torre. It is a tower. Also, we have an elephant—that is our animal. But we are best known for the Torre symbol."

"Okay," I said. "But what does this have to do with Marco calling the café poison?"

Gia sighed. "It is very difficult for tourists to understand all of the emotions behind the Palio," she explained. "It is very, very serious . . . this horse race. It is not like any horse race anywhere else in the world! We—all the *contrade*—prepare for the Palio all year long. It is what we live for, here in Siena. To win? That is the highest honor of all!"

"Wow," I commented. "I've never heard of anything like this in my life!"

"Me, either," Miss O commented. "Is it more important than soccer?" she asked. "Because I know soccer is really, really popular in Italy."

"Sì, it is even more important than soccer." Gia replied.

"Oh, boy!" Miss O said.

"So, you see," Gia went on, "there is so much competition among the contrade. And for the Torre and the Tartuca? For many years, these two contrade have been rivals. It is a long, long story . . . this feud. So for Marco to go into a café owned by a Tartuca is unheard of!"

"Really?" Juliette asked.

Gia nodded. "Really," she replied. "Marco is very serious about the Palio. I am, too—all of us in my family are. But I do not take the feud as seriously as my brother. True, I would never marry out of my contrada, and I don't have any close friends from other contrade, but I will shop in stores and go to cafés in all of Siena. No matter what contrada the owners come from."

We all exchanged stunned looks. No friends from outside your neighborhood? How unbelievable is that? I mean, if we had the Palio back at home, none of us could be friends because we all live in different neighborhoods! Well, except for Miss O, Juliette, and Isabella. They live only a couple of blocks away from each other.

As we pulled down the long, dirt road leading to Gia's family estate, I sat back and absorbed the importance of what Gia was saying. The Palio was unlike anything I had ever experienced! I could never imagine living in a place where neighborhoods competed so seriously against each other all year. It was so weird!

As we pulled up to the estate, the girls and I were shocked to see that Gia's family lived in a mansion! Actually, it was a mansion made up of a few large structures: the main estate, a carriage house, a guest house, and the stables. Gia said there was also a vineyard, a swimming pool, a lake, and a beautiful garden on the property.

"Holy cannoli!" Harlie exclaimed as we got out of the minivan.

"You can say that again," Juliette muttered.

"Wow, Gia!" Isabella said. "Is your family rich?"

Gia laughed. "My padre," she explained. "He is of Italian nobility. His family, for many generations, has been part of high society in Siena. Hundreds of years ago it meant a lot more, but these days, it is really just an honorary title."

As she spoke, an older man in a polo shirt, shorts and sandals stepped out of the main house. He saw us standing with Gia and he waved.

"Papà!" Gia called out to him. "Come to meet my friends!"

Gia's father looked nothing like what I'd imagined a "noble" would look like. He looked more like my Grandpa Joel than anything! In fact, I think my Grandpa Joel had the same exact polo shirt.

"This is my *papà*," Gia told us. "Franco Reganato. Papà, this is

Justine, the general's daughter, and her very best friends: Harlie, Miss O, Juliette, and Isabella."

Franco Reganato's booming loud voice startled us.

"*Piacere!*" he announced.

Gia laughed. "He says, 'It's nice to meet you!'"

"It's nice to meet you, too, sir," I replied. (Being a general's daughter, I've always been super-polite to adults.)

"Sir?" he replied. "Please, call me 'Papà'!"

Harlie giggled. "Okay, Papà!" she said. "Your estate is beautiful!"

"*Grazie,* Harlie! Or is it Isabella?" he asked.

"No, you were right the first time. I'm Harlie," Harlie replied. "How do you say, 'You're welcome' in Italian?" she asked Gia.

"*Prego,*" Gia told her.

"Prego!" Harlie said to Gia's father.

"Would you like to see the estate?" Papa Reganato asked us.

We all nodded eagerly.

"But please, can we first meet Scroscio?" Isabella asked.

Gia's father's whole face lit up when Isabella mentioned Scroscio.

"*Certo!* Of course! I would love to introduce you to my Scroscio! I see Gia has told you all about the Palio?"

We nodded. "Yes, she did," I told him. "And how Scroscio will win!"

Papa Reganato laughed very loudly. "Win the Palio?" he cried. "You bet your life!"

We followed Gia's father toward the stables as he told us more about the Palio and about the feud among the contrade.

"Do you want to know why we have this feud?" he asked us.

I nodded eagerly. "Yes! Please tell us!" I asked.

"Well, the feud began twenty-five years ago," he explained. "That summer, the Torre had a magnificent horse entered in the Palio. Her name was Argia. Like my Gia."

"Gia is short for Argia," Gia piped in.

"So our Argia was the pride of the Torre," Gia's father went on. "She was so fast! The fastest horse I ever raised. Well, until my Scroscio that is! Anyway, on the day of the race, Argia looked great. We have a few trial races in the morning, to put the horses in the mood for competition, and Argia won first every time!"

"Wow!" Miss O said. "That's great!"

"Yes. But even greater was that during the actual Palio, Argia came in first place! The judges announced her the winner, and suddenly there was a big uproar from the Tartuca. They were yelling and screaming, 'No fair! No fair!'"

"What happened?" Juliette asked.

"They claimed that *their* horse was the winner, and that the Torre cheated!" Papa Reganato told us. I could see the anger in his eyes and hear it in his voice as he remembered the race that day.

"No way!" Harlie exclaimed.

"Yes, I'm sorry to say," he replied. "And to this day, the Tartuca claim to have won that Palio—even though the Torre were awarded the winning banner. Every year, the Tartuca blame us for cheating. It is a crime, to hear them say that!"

"That is terrible!" I agreed.

"More terrible is that since that win twenty-five years ago," he told us, "the Torre have not won another Palio! It has disappointed our contrada very much. We are really hoping to win this year."

"No, Papà! We *will* win this year!" a voice called to us.

To our surprise, Marco was already at the stables, brushing his horse's magnificent light brown mane.

"Buon giorno!" Marco called out when he saw us.

"Hi, Marco," I said.

Marco smiled as he presented Scroscio to us. "This is Scroscio!" he exclaimed proudly.

Isabella's eyes were wide with glee. "Wow! She is beautiful!" she proclaimed. "Bella!"

"Scroscio will win back our honor!" Marco went on. "And put the Tartuca back in their place!"

"Your father told us about the feud," I said to Marco. "I think we now understand why you hate the café so much."

"Sì. I am sorry to be like that last night. Especially when I just met you for the first time. That is not what I am like. It's just that when it comes to the Palio and the Tartuca, I get . . . *pazzo!* Crazy!"

We all giggled.

"That's okay," I told him. "We get it now."

"Your father told us that the Tartuca call the Torre cheaters," Miss O said. "That's terrible! They are sore losers, I think."

Gia nodded. "Yes, we think so, too."

"Papà, did you tell the girls about the *Parata del Palio*?" Marco asked.

"Not yet," Marco's father replied.

Marco's eyes shone as he told us about the Parata del Palio—the Parade of the Palio—that the Torre put on every year, the night before the big race.

"We drape our horse in the banner from our last win, and we parade her along the Piazza del Campo!" he explained excitedly. "This, we believe, will bring our horse good luck!"

"Sounds fun!" I told him. "You still have the banner from twenty-five years ago?" I asked.

Marco's eyes widened. "But of course!" he replied. "It is the Torre's most prized possession!" he added. "We have it hanging proudly on display in the *Museo della Torre!*"

"A museum?" Harlie asked.

Marco nodded. "Yes, The Torre Museum."

"*Good figuring!*" I whispered to Harlie.

Harlie grinned at me.

"*Sì!* We have a museum filled with everything from the Palio and the *contrada della Torre* . We have pictures, portraits, the *palios*—banners— we have won throughout history. We even have some locks of hair from our winning horses!"

"Really?" Miss O asked. "Cool. Can we see the museum? Is it far from here?"

Marco gazed up at his father. "Papà? Can I take the girls to the Museo della Torre?" he asked.

"Of course!" Papa Reganato replied. "I think we have enough bicycles for everyone. Why don't you ride there?"

We followed Marco from the stables to the large garage next to the main house. When he led us inside, we were surprised to see that indeed the Reganatos *did* have a lot of bicycles! We each had our own to ride!

It was only a fifteen-minute bicycle ride to the Torre Museum. As we rode, I thought about how much fun and excitement I was having in Italy already—and it had only been less than twenty-four hours since we'd arrived! I hoped my friends were having a good time, too.

The Torre Museum was a white stucco building on a city street with other stucco buildings that looked sort of official-like. Marco rested his bicycle against the side of the building and we all did the same. Then we followed him inside.

The first thing I noticed in the museum was a large flag hanging from the ceiling. I knew right away it was the flag of the contrada della Torre because of the elephant and the tower emblem on the flag.

"See the elephant and the tower?" I asked my friends. "Gia said they were the symbols of the Torre."

"Is that the banner?" Miss O asked Marco, pointing to the flag.

Marco shook his head. "No, that is just our emblem. The banner— the *palio*—is like a trophy. Every year a famous artist from Siena is asked to design the official palio. The official palio is what is given to the winning horse. As I explained before, the last palio banner the Torre won twenty-five years ago is kept in an honored place on the back wall. It is most beautiful! Come! I will show it to you!"

Excitedly, we followed Marco through the museum. (He was right about the horse hair on display. Truth? I thought it was a little gross, to be honest!). We passed paintings of horses, saddles in display cases, posters from the Palio, and photographs. Marco wasn't kidding when he said the Torre have saved every memento from past years of the Palio.

"Look, Miss O!" I said. "That must be a picture of Argia wearing the winning palio—"

All of a sudden, we heard a loud cry of anguish.

"*Oh, mamma mia!*"

It was Marco!

We raced ahead to find him staring up at a blank spot on the museum wall.

"*Il palio!*" he cried, before shouting a whole bunch of words in Italian.

We didn't need to know Italian to figure out what was going on.

The Torre's winning palio . . . was gone!

Chapter 6
Stolen Banner

"The Tartuca!" Marco cried. "They are responsible for stealing our banner!"

"Are you sure it was hanging here?" Harlie asked him.

Marco shot her a look.

"Okay. Never mind. You're sure," Harlie said.

"Well, let's think this through, Marco," I said diplomatically. "Before you blame the Tartuca for stealing, let's rule out everything else. Could it have been taken down to be cleaned or something?"

Marco shook his head. "No! Never!"

"Um, okay. What about someone from the Torre?" I suggested. "Could someone else have taken it to get it ready for Scroscio to wear in the Parade of the Palio?"

"No!" Marco insisted. "Nobody would take the palio without asking me or Papà first!" He spun around and shouted for Roberto, the man who worked at the museum and who had let us in. Roberto came racing over and gasped loudly when he saw the bare wall. The two shouted some more in Italian, then Roberto ran off.

"I must call my father!" Marco said.

"Here. You can use my cell."

Marco grabbed the cell from me. "Papà will be so angry! I will call Gia first," he said.

Seconds later, Marco was in a heated discussion with Gia on the phone. We all stood around him, not understanding a word, but feeling anxious and nervous anyway. Finally, Marco snapped off the cell.

"Please," he said. "Let's go home. Gia and I must tell Papà about the banner."

As we rode back to the estate (raced in warp speed was more like it!), Miss O rode up alongside of me.

"Do you really think the other contrada would break into the museum and steal the banner?" she asked.

I knew it sounded incredible, but then again, this whole Palio thing was bizarre. Gia, Marco, and even their father seemed super-serious about it all.

I shrugged as I peddled. "I don't know," I told Miss O. "It sounds like a silly sort of thing to do over a horse race. But what do I know?"

"This is why I hate the Tartuca so much!" Marco called to us as he rode. "They play dirty! They steal! The Torre would never steal! Never!"

Miss O and I exchanged looks.

Because we had ridden so crazy-quickly back to the estate, we made it back in ten minutes instead of fifteen. We returned our bicycles to the garage, then followed Marco into the main house. Gia was waiting for us, and, as I'd imagined, she was consumed with worry—just like Marco.

The girls and I stood in the grand foyer of the main house while Gia and Marco whispered frantically. I felt bad for them—no one likes to have something stolen from them—but I really couldn't figure out what all the fuss was about. Scroscio could still race, couldn't she?

Finally, Papa Reganato came down the staircase.

"*Ciao belle!*" he said happily. "Hello, beautiful ladies! How did you enjoy our museum?"

Before we could answer, Marco stepped up to his father.

"Papà! *Notizie cattive!*" he said urgently.

"*Very* bad news," Gia added.

Her father's face fell as she explained to him what we'd found at the museum. I was so surprised as I watched Papa Reganato's usual jolly expression turn completely sour! He barely said a word to us—instead he stormed off, ranting in Italian.

"He is going to call the *polizia*," Gia explained.

"The police?" Harlie exclaimed. "Really? Because of a stolen banner?"

It was all so unbelievable.

"I told you," Gia said solemnly, "we take the Palio very seriously."

"But the banner being stolen," I said, "shouldn't affect Scroscio in the race, right?"

"Well, no," Gia replied. "But without the banner, Scroscio will not have our good luck in the Parata del Palio."

"But that's just a superstition," Miss O pointed out.

"Yes, but we take it very, very seriously," Gia reminded her. "Every person in the Torre will be disheartened if Scroscio can't march in the Parata."

"Wow," Miss O muttered. "This is really terrible then! What can we do to help?"

"Yes! We'd really like to help, Gia," Isabella said.

Juliette, Harlie and I nodded.

"What can we do?" I asked.

Gia frowned. "I'm sorry, but I don't think there is anything you can do. This is a very sad day for the Torre," she added glumly. "I really should take you back to the residenza."

My father was able to meet us back at the residenza at lunchtime, so Gia dropped us off and headed back to her family. We felt so bad for her and Marco! I know we'd just met them both yesterday, but they were already like old friends.

Upstairs, we filled my dad in on the stolen banner and all. He, too, couldn't believe that someone would steal the banner, but when we told him how Papa Reganato had called the police, he agreed the whole ordeal must be a lot more serious that we could understand.

"Well, I still have some work to finish on my laptop," Dad told us, "but how about some lunch?"

"Ooh! Can we go down to the café?" I asked suddenly. "Can we, Dad? Can we eat lunch there?"

My friends looked at me in confusion.

"But we're supposed to hate that café now," Miss O reminded me. "It's Tartuca, remember?"

"I know!" I said. "But I was just thinking. Maybe we should go down there and hang out for a while. Try to get some information about the Tartuca. Maybe even see if someone mentions the stolen banner!"

Juliette's eyes lit up at the possibility of investigating. It was no secret that Juliette dreamed of becoming a reporter when she grew up, so investigating was right up her alley!

"Great idea!" she exclaimed. "I'm up for some investigating!"

"Can we, Dad?" I asked again.

My father rubbed his chin, considering the idea. Finally, he nodded. "Sure," he said. "I suppose a little spying can't hurt. It's for a good cause, anyway," he added.

"Thanks, Dad!" I said, giving him a big hug. "You can bring your laptop there, too, because they have free Wi-Fi. I saw a sign."

"Now *that's* what I call investigating," Juliette commended me. "You'd make a great reporter, Justine!"

I grinned. "Thanks! Let's go!"

Downstairs, we found two empty tables at the café, indoors. We each grabbed a seat at one just as an older boy came by to hand us menus. My father sat at the other empty table and set up his laptop.

"*Benvenute!*" the boy said cheerfully. "*Mi chiamo Antonio. Desiderano?*" He smiled at us, waiting for us to say something.

"Um, we don't know what you just said," Harlie told him.

"Ah! Do you speak English?" he asked.

We nodded.

"And you, too?" he asked me.

I nodded and he shook his head. "I thought you must be an Italian girl," he said. "You dress just like an Italian fashion model."

I beamed and touched my silk scarf with my hand. "Cool! Thank you! Grazie!"

"So I said, 'Welcome! My name is Antonio', just before. May I help you?'"

Isabella smiled. "That's what I thought you said. I understood some of it," she said proudly.

"Wow, you know Italian?" he asked.

"We're trying to learn some while we are here," I explained.

"Are you from the United States?" Antonio asked.

"Yes, we live in Westchester. That's in New York," Miss O told him.

"Near New York City?" Antonio asked.

"I live in New York City!" Harlie exclaimed. "On the Upper West Side."

"Then it is a pleasure to meet you beautiful girls from New York!" Antonio said.

I blushed a little, feeling as though he were flirting with us big time! "Do you live in Siena?" I asked him.

"Sì! All my life I live here. My papà owns this café," he added.

The girls and I exchanged inconspicuous looks. He was definitely part of the Tartuca then!

"Wait! I want to give you some *dolci*!" He left for a minute, then returned with a plate of the most delicious-looking Italian pastries! Harlie's eyes nearly popped out of her head.

"Wow!" she exclaimed when he placed the big plate of pastries in front of her. "But what do you have for everyone else?" she joked.

"Heh-heh," Miss O chuckled. "Let me have some of that *torta al cioccolata*," she said. "It looks a lot better than the one I make at home!"

Juliette eyed her younger sister. "Miss O, how do you know what that is called in Italian?" she asked.

Miss O waved her off. "Oh, please!" she said. "Baking is a universal language!"

"These cookies are delish," Isabella told Antonio.

"*Sì, deliziosi*," Antonio said with a grin. "Everybody in Siena loves my father's café."

Well, not everybody, I told myself, thinking about Marco and the Reganatos.

"Can I ask you something, Antonio?" Juliette asked.

"*Sì?*"

"These flags, hanging all around the café," she said. "With tortoises on them. What are they for? Do you like tortoises or something?"

Wow! Juliette sure sounded as if she had no idea what they were!

Antonio's eyes widened and so did his smile. "Well, *sì!* I love tortoises! But this is not why we have the flags with tartucas all over our café. They are for the Palio."

We all pretended we had never heard of the Palio before.

"What's that?" Juliette asked.

"You don't know what is the Palio?" Antonio asked incredibly. "You are not here in Siena for the Palio?"

"We are here in Siena because my father is working here this summer," I explained, pointing to my father at the next table. "We just got here last night."

Antonio then pulled off his waiter's apron and flung it over a chair. Then he took an empty seat at our table.

"Well! Then I must be the one to tell you all about the Palio!" he declared. "You cannot be in Siena in the summer and not know about the Palio!"

Funny, I thought, *that was exactly what Gia had told us right in this very café last night! But we hadn't met Antonio last night—I guess he wasn't working.*

Antonio began to explain to us the history of the Palio and the contrade, only his version had a few differences from the one we already knew. For instance, Antonio insisted that his contrada was the best contrada and that the Tartuca horse would be the Palio winner this summer!

"When was the last time the Tartuca won the banner?" Juliette asked.

At that moment, Antonio's expression completely changed. "Twenty-five years ago!" he told us. "We won the Palio twenty-five years ago, but another contrada cheated, and we were not awarded the banner!"

"That's terrible!" Miss O said, giving me a little kick under the table.

"Sì," Antonio said with a sigh. "But that will never happen again!" he added defiantly. "In fact, next week I know the Tartuca horse will win the Palio!"

I bit my bottom lip. "How do you know that?" I asked suspiciously.

"Our *fantino,* our jockey, is one of the fastest jockeys in all of Italy!" Antonio said. "He is sure to win, especially before the cheating Torre!"

I felt like jumping up and yelling at Antonio, "The Torre did not cheat!" but I stopped myself. I reminded myself we were there to gather information and not cause another feud . . . between the Tartuca and . . . the *Westchester!*

"And," Antonio added, suddenly leaning in toward the center of the table and lowering his voice to a whisper, "I know for sure that we will win the Palio this year!" He grinned at us mysteriously.

"I've made sure of it!"

Chapter 7
Five *Belle* Italian Spies!

The very next morning, I got ready before anyone else. I wanted to be the first one to greet Gia when she came for us, and tell her what we found out last night: that Marco was right! The Tartuca had stolen the Torre banner!

We couldn't believe our ears when Antonio told us he "made sure" that the Tartuca would win the Palio. Miss O had kicked me under the table (she'd been doing that all night!), and I was just glad she was wearing her squishy, soft Floaties flip-flops, because I was starting to get bruised legs.

Last night we sat up talking for a long time about the Palio and about our new friends, Gia and Marco. They were so, so nice! We all agreed we would do whatever we could to help them.

As I waited quietly in the living room for Gia, I passed the time by loading a new roll of film into my 35-millimeter camera. It isn't so easy to do—you have to get the holes on the film lined up perfectly with the spokes inside the film feed. Anyway, I wanted to do it to have a fresh roll of film for today. As I was working, my father came in all dressed for work.

"Are you girls all ready?" he asked, looking surprised to see me up and dressed at "oh-seven-hundred-hours" (7 A.M.).

"No, just me," I told him. "I wanted to be the one to tell Gia about last night and the Tartuca boy from the café."

"That's very nice of you, Justine. I'm glad you like Gia and her brother."

"They are so great!" I told him. "We just feel bad about the banner being stolen. We want to help them find it."

"I wish I could help, too," my father said. "But there's not much I can do to help find a missing banner—from my office desk. But keep me up-to-date on your troop's progress."

"Yes, sir!" I told him.

"Now, what about breakfast? Do you think the girls would enjoy Italian pancakes again?" he asked with a grin. "Or, I also make great Italian waffles and Italian omelets!"

I laughed. "Maybe just cereal today, Dad," I told him. "Something we can gobble up quickly to be ready to go when Gia comes. The earlier the better," I added. "We have a plan!"

My father's eyes narrowed. "A plan? Hmmm. A 'search and recovery' mission, I assume?"

I nodded. "Something like that," I said. "Definitely the 'search' part. And we hope the 'recovery' part, too!"

Just then we heard a soft knock on the door to the residenza. It was Gia. I let her in and invited her into the living room.

"Buon giorno. I am early today?" Gia asked. "I felt so bad cutting our day short yesterday."

"Was the Torre banner found?" I asked hopefully.

Gia shook her head disappointedly. "No, I am sad to say. The polizia are investigating. But it is very difficult. They cannot question the thousands of people from the contrada della Tartuca!"

"Well, I think I know where they can start!" I declared.

Gia gazed at me in concern. "*Come?*" she asked. "Pardon? What do you mean?"

I moved closer on the sofa to Gia. "We—the girls and I—have some good news," I told her. "Well, the news itself is not *good* news, but it *is* good that we found it!"

"Sì?"

"Okay," I began. "Yesterday, after you dropped us off, we went to the café for lunch. The Tartuca café that Marco hates."

"My brother shouldn't have told you about his strong feelings about the café!" Gia insisted. "He is too emotional when it comes to the Palio! But he never should have soured you and your friends about the café. It is rather lovely."

"But I think Marco was right!" I exclaimed.

Gia's eyes widened, just as the girls came into the room.

"Did you tell her about Antonio yet?" Harlie asked.

"I'm about to," I replied.

"Hi, Gia!" Juliette said. "Buon giorno!"

Gia smiled. "Sì! Buon giorno, Signorina Julietta! Come stai?"

Juliette looked at me for help.

I shrugged. "Don't look at me!" I told her. "I don't know what she said!"

Gia laughed. "I said, 'Good morning, Miss Juliette,'" she told us.

"And you said, 'How are you?'" Isabella piped in. "Right?"

Gia nodded. "Sì! 'Come stai?' is Italian for 'How are you?'"

"Come stai," Juliette repeated. "Come stai. But how do I answer?" she asked.

"Well, how are you?" Gia asked her.

Juliette smiled. "I'm great!" she replied. "Really great!"

"So then you reply, Sto bene!"

"Awesome. Sto bene!" Juliette repeated.

"Me, too!" Miss O chimed in. "Sto bene!"

"And I'm hungry," Harlie added.

We all laughed. "You're always hungry," I commented.

"You say, Ho fame," Gia told her. "That is, 'I'm hungry.'"

"Ho really, really fame!" Harlie exclaimed.

Again, we all laughed. "Can you wait five more minutes, Harlie?" I asked. "I was just telling Gia about yesterday at the café, and I was at the really good part."

Harlie nodded. "Yeah, sure!"

I turned back to Gia. "So, I think Marco was right about the Tartuca stealing the banner," I said. "Because we started talking to this boy

Antonio, who said his father owned the café. And then Juliette asked him about the tortoise flags around the café. We pretended we didn't know anything about the Palio."

Gia's eyes widened. She smiled. "So you were *spiase*?"

"Spiase?" I repeated. "Oh! You mean spies? Then, yeah! I guess we were!"

"It is so nice for you to do that for the Torre," she said. "You are great friends to the Torre. I shall ask Papà to name you honorary members of the Torre!"

I beamed, and the girls and I exchanged excited looks. "That would be so cool," I said.

"Tell her what happened next," Miss O urged.

"Right. Okay, so we were *spying*," I went on, "and Juliette asked about the flags, and then Antonio sat down at our table and began to tell us about the Palio and the Tartuca. That's when I asked him if they ever won, and he told us exactly what Marco said: that the Tartuca believe the Torre cheated twenty-five years ago, and that their horse really won!"

"All lies! This is not true." Gia exclaimed.

"But that wasn't the best part," I went on. "Antonio told us that he is positive the Tartuca will win the Palio this year. His exact words were, 'I made sure of it!'"

Gia gasped. "I can't believe he told you this!" she cried. "You are right! This means he has our palio!"

My father interrupted us as he came into the living room with some cereal boxes, milk, and five bowls. "Now, Justine," he said diplomatically, "I don't think it's a good idea to get Gia's hopes up about this boy from the café having the missing banner."

"But, Dad!" I protested. "I told you what he said!"

"Yes, I know," my father replied. "And you're probably right. This boy *probably* has something to do with the banner. But you don't know this for sure."

Well, I *felt* like I knew it for sure, but I suppose my father was right.

"Yeah, I guess," I said.

"So what should we do?" Harlie asked as she fixed herself a bowl of cereal with fresh blueberries on top.

We all looked at each other.

"I have an idea!" Juliette suddenly announced. We turned our gazes in her direction.

"What is it, Juje?" Miss O asked. "Juje" is Miss O's nickname for her sister. It's pronounced, "*Joo-gee*."

"Well, Marco said that every contrada has a museum, right?" she asked. We all nodded.

"All of the seventeen *contrade* have a museum in Siena," Gia verified for us.

"Okay, so I was thinking," Juliette went on, sounding like a true investigative reporter, "what if we went to the Tartuca museum? We could keep pretending we were just tourists and didn't know anything, and have a look around. We could look for clues—maybe even find the banner!"

"Juliette, that's a *great* idea!" I exclaimed. I spun around to face my father. "Dad? Can we?" I asked.

"Only if you go with Gia," he replied.

"This will be a problem," Gia said, interrupting. "I cannot go to the Tartuca museum. They will know I am from Torre. My family is a well-known Torre family."

I groaned. "But it was such a good plan," I commented.

"What if Gia drives us there," Miss O suggested, "and then she can wait in the car outside for us?"

I brightened, feeling sure my father would allow that. "Dad?" I asked hopefully.

My father thought about it for a minute, then he finally nodded. "I think that will be fine," he said. "Just as long as you stick together—nobody breaks rank."

"Right! We will stick together! I promise!"

"And I will wait right outside for the girls," Gia added. "We will have our cells, too."

The rest of us filled our bowls with cereal and chowed down as quickly as we could. (Harlie had *two* bowls!) We left the residenza shortly after my father, and after promising another million times that we would behave like good little soldiers and not break rank.

Gia drove us to the Tartuca museum, which was only a few minutes away from the residenza. She explained to us as she drove that all the neighborhoods in Siena are very close to one another and that they are all pretty much off their own roads, all of which lead to the heart of Siena: the Piazza del Campo.

When we arrived at the neighborhood, we searched the building façades to see which of them was the museum. I was the one who spotted the big flag atop a gray-stoned building. The image of a tortoise caught my eye almost instantly: the emblem of the Tartuca.

"Sì. This is it," Gia said. "I will remain in the car on the side of the building right here. You girls go in through the front."

"This is so exciting!" Miss O exclaimed. "I feel like a spy for real!"

"An Italian spy," I added.

"A beautiful Italian spy!" Juliette corrected.

"Well, I have to admit that I'm a bit nervous," Harlie commented.

I nodded. "I think we all are," I told her. The others agreed. "But there's nothing to be nervous about," I added. "For all anyone knows, we are here as tourists checking out a museum in Siena. That's all."

"Okay," Isabella said, taking in a deep breath, then letting it out. "Let's go!"

Together we headed toward the museum and through the glass double doors into the lobby. Like the Torre museum, the Tartuca museum was nothing fancy. But it sure was crowded—packed with so many posters and flags and photographs! I pulled my own camera out of its camera bag and removed the lens cap.

Moments after we entered the museum an older woman appeared from nowhere.

"Buon giorno!" she called out to us. "Benvenute! Come state?"

Harlie opened her mouth to answer, but I nudged her just in time. *"We're supposed to be tourists!"* I reminded her. *"Tourists who don't speak Italian!"*

"Right!" she whispered back.

"Uh, so what did you say?" she said loudly to the woman. "Are you talking to us? We don't speak Italian. We are just tourists. Tourists who don't speak Italian. At all."

I nudged Harlie again. *"Too much,"* I whispered.

"Okay, sorry," she whispered back.

"Ah! So you don't speak *Italiano*?" the woman asked.

"Nope. Not a word. Like I said," Harlie replied.

"Well, we know a *few* words," Isabella said gently. I could tell she was trying to warm up to the woman.

"Where are you from?" the woman asked.

"From the residenza," Harlie replied. "It's not far from here, by the Piazza—"

"I think she means where is *home*," I pointed out.

Harlie laughed. "Oh! Sorry! We're from New York," she said.

"Very nice!" the woman said. "My name is Etta Servi, and I will be pleased to show you the Tartuca museum."

We smiled, then followed her as she started our tour with the history of the Palio, which dated back to 1651. It was pretty interesting, and I had to remind myself why we were there in the first place. I took the lens cap off my camera and started clicking away, looking for clues as I clicked. I also kept a keen eye out for the banner itself. Wouldn't it be just awesome if we found the banner here and stole it back?

I daydreamed for a second of bringing the missing banner back to the Torre. Papa Reganato would probably have a parade in *our* honor! Maybe even declare the day, "The Day of the Westchester Girls"!

Back to reality.

Like the Torre museum, the Tartuca museum held many artifacts from past Palio races. They, too, had a lock of hair taken from the mane of a winning horse. The woman said that particular horse had raced in 1902!

That was when Juliette asked Etta Servi the question that changed everything.

"When was the last time a Tartuca horse won the Palio?" she asked.

Right before our eyes, as if she had been suddenly transformed, Etta Servi's manner went from pleasant . . . to ruffled! Her cheeks turned red, and she began to speak passionately.

"The Tartuca horse was cheated out of a win twenty-five years ago!" she declared.

I bit my bottom lip. "Uh, what do you mean?" I asked innocently.

Etta waved us over to a glass display case in the center of the museum. In it sat a worn-out saddle and a pair of reigns. "This was from our horse. Her name was Primo. She was a very, very fast horse. And oh, so bella!" She pointed to a large photograph hanging on the wall behind us.

Isabella agreed. "Yes! Sì!" she said. "Primo was beautiful!"

"So what happened?" Juliette asked.

"It was a scandal," she said. "Just terrible. Look closely," she instructed. "At the photograph. The horses are crossing the finish line. The horse next to Primo is a horse from another contrada. From the Torre."

I didn't like the way Etta Servi said "Torre." She made it seem like it was a bad word or something. Juliette immediately shot me a look that said, "*Omigod!*" I nodded in her direction to show her I agreed with her reaction.

"You see how close the two horses are?" Etta pointed out. "But it is clear who the winner is. The winner was Primo!" she declared. "But the judges didn't agree. Don't you agree Primo was the winner?"

Harlie shrugged.

"I think—" Miss O began.

Etta shook her head and cut Miss O off. "The Torre cheated. They must have paid the judge money to declare their horse the winner."

None of us said anything.

"But anyone will tell you—except people from the contrada della Torre—that it was Primo who won the Palio!" Etta said finally.

Isabella inspected the photo closely. Her nose was practically touching the paper. "Well, Mrs. Servi, they *do* look awfully close," she pointed out. "But this is a difficult angle to tell for sure."

Etta shook her head again. "It is indeed hard to tell from the photograph," she said. "But I was there. I saw it with my own two eyes. Our Primo was clearly the winner!"

"Primo was ridden by the Tartuca's fastest jockey!" Etta went on, without even looking at us. "She was trained in America!"

"Maybe we had better go," I suggested quietly. Etta seemed lost in her memory of that day.

"Yeah," Miss O agreed. "I think it's time to go. *Did you spot the banner?*" she asked me in a whisper.

"*No! I didn't see it anywhere!*" I replied. "*And I was really, really hoping we'd find it here.*"

"*Me, too,*" Miss O said glumly.

"Uh, thank you! Grazie, Signora Servi!" I said. "But we have to get going. Our tour guide is waiting for us."

Etta nodded and gave us half a smile. I think she had totally tired herself out going on and on about Primo!

We headed for the double doors as quickly as we could. Juliette nudged me as we walked. "*Should we snoop some more?*" she whispered.

"I don't know," I replied nervously. "My father said to be careful."

"Just take some pictures on your way out," Juliette urged. "Secretly."

I lifted my camera nervously. I could try to just snap some pictures without Etta Servi seeing. But just as I lifted my camera, Antonio burst through the front door to the museum and saw me!

"Hey!" he said, when he recognized me. I noticed he was carrying a large burlap sack, which he covered protectively with his arm.

"Oh, hi!" I said awkwardly. "It's you!"

"Oh, hello! You are from the café last night!" he said.

I nodded. "Um, yes! But we were just leaving!" I told him.

He stared at us in what I thought was a suspicious manner. "What are you doing here?" he asked. "At this museum for Tartuca?"

The girls and I exchanged nervous glances.

"Oh, well, we thought what you told us last night about the horse race was so *cool!*" I managed to choke out. "We wanted to come see it for ourselves!"

"We're tourists!" Harlie piped in. "We don't speak Italian!"

I shot her a look.

"We, um . . . we were, uh, just passing by," I sputtered, "on our way to Vinci. Yes! That's where we're going today with our guide. To Leonardo da Vinci's hometown. For sightseeing."

"But how did you find our Tartuca museum?" Antonio asked me.

I tried to remain calm, but his question made me nervous. How *did* I know where to find the museum? How was I going to explain *that*? I mean, it's not like the contrada museums are on tourist maps.

Luckily, Juliette came to my rescue. "It's the funniest thing!" she said. "We were driving by, like Justine said, and we saw the tortoise flag on top of the building. We noticed it right away, because you have them all over your café, so we came in to check it out!"

Wow, Juliette! Good thinking! I said to her in my head.

Antonio broke into a grin. "Sì! Our Tartuca flag!"

Before Juliette could continue, a loud car horn honked on the street outside.

Honk! Honk!

I spun around and could see Gia's white minivan. Gia was waiting for us out in front of the museum. "Oh! There's our guide!" I said, glad for an opportunity to stop talking to Antonio and leave the museum. "We really gotta go! Nice to see you again, Antonio! *Arriverderci!*"

"Arriv——" Antonio began. He stopped in mid-sentence. I noticed he was staring out the double doors and into the white minivan.

"Wait one minute!" he cried out in alarm. "She is your guide? I know her! She is from the Torre!"

I gulped. We all stood there, unable to move or to say anything. I felt like a deer in the road, caught in a car's headlights at night.

Chapter 8

Whose Side Are You On Anyway?

"Um, she is just our guide!" I cried, finally finding my voice. "We are just out sightseeing! Like I told you before!" My mouth felt dry as I spoke and all I wanted to do was get out of that museum!

"That is Argia Reganato!" Antonio insisted. "She is a noble from the contrada della Torre! You must have known this! Did she ask you to come here?"

I shook my head. "No, Antonio. We told her we wanted to stop and see it when we drove by and saw the flag. Like Juliette said. She didn't want to come inside and said she would wait for us in the car. That's all."

I could tell by his expression that he didn't believe me. But I was through spying for the day—I wanted O-U-T!

"We really have to go," I said flatly. "It was nice to see you again, Antonio. Bye!"

I grabbed Miss O's arm and pulled her through the double doors and onto the sidewalk. The other girls followed closely behind. I could feel Antonio's eyes on us as we piled into the minivan.

"Go!" I cried out to Gia. "Go! Drive away! Please!"

Gia stepped on the gas and the car lurched forward. "What is it?" she asked. "What happened in there? Did you find our banner?"

"No, I'm sorry, we didn't see the banner," I told her, still out of breath from all the excitement. "But *we* got found out," I added. "Antonio saw you in the car and he knows who you are."

"He was really acting suspicious," Harlie said.

"More like *conspicuous*," Juliette commented.

"What do you mean?" I asked her.

"Come on! Didn't you see that big sack he had with him?" she asked.

I nodded. I'd almost bumped into that sack on the way out of the museum. He *was* acting a little weird about the sack, I had noticed.

"I bet I know what was in that sack!" Juliette stated matter-of-factly.

We were all silent in the van.

"Are you thinking what I'm thinking?" Miss O asked her sister.

"Sì," Juliette replied. "I'm thinking Antonio had the stolen Torre banner in that sack!"

From the Tartuca museum we headed to Gia's estate to pick up Marco. Gia's brother was joining us that morning on a short trip to the town of Vinci, where the famous artist Leonardo da Vinci was from. Vinci wasn't far from Siena at all, and we were pretty excited to visit the da Vinci Museum that was there. In addition to being a painter, Leonardo da Vinci was also a scientist and an inventor. The museum, my father had told me, was filled with models of the crazy things he'd designed and invented, including flying machines and water lifts.

The second Marco stepped into the van, we all started talking at once, telling him about Antonio and what had happened at the Tartuca museum. Marco's eyes were wide as he listened. We tried to remember everything Antonio said and did as we relayed the information to Marco.

"This museum woman is wrong!" Marco insisted, when we told him the story Etta Servi had told us about the Palio twenty-five years ago. "The Torre horse won fair and square!"

"Every year the Tartuca protests our win from that race," Gia added, shaking her head in dismay. "It's the same thing every summer at Palio time. They tell everyone we cheated and that their horse was really the winner."

"They have a photograph of the finish line at the museum," Isabella told them. "And she kept insisting Primo was the clear winner. But really, you couldn't tell anything from that picture."

"I was a little girl at the time of that race," Gia told us. "Four years, maybe five. The Torre horse was from my father's stables. I remember this because the horse was named Argia, after me! And I remember standing on the closest terrazzo to the finish line and watching as Argia won the race. I saw her win! I will never forget that!"

"The judges believed this, too!" Marco added. "And their word is final!"

"So do you think the missing banner might be in that sack Antonio was carrying?" Harlie asked Marco as we drove.

"Maybe," he replied. "You say the sack was big?" he asked us.

I nodded. "Yes. Pretty big."

"I told you before—the Tartuca play dirty," Marco said. "This is why I think that our banner is in that sack. I believe the Tartuca stole our banner so Scroscio would not have it for the Parata del Palio."

"So what are you going to do?" I asked Marco.

He looked me square in the eye. "Whatever I have to do," he told me, "to get the Torre banner back to the Torre!"

At the da Vinci Museum, all we did was come up with plans to steal back the banner. Some of them made sense—like when Harlie suggested we just *ask* Antonio for the banner back!!!—but some of them were downright silly, like when Miss O thought we could climb up on the roof of the Tartuca museum and lower one of us through a window. It's true, she's seen *Mission: Impossible* many times, but I think her imagination was really getting the best of her!

Or maybe she was inspired by all the designs and drawings that were on display in the Leonardo da Vinci museum. Some of them were so wacky! Like the drawings he had constructed for a "sequin-making machine." It was nuts! Now I know this is the guy who painted the famous *Mona Lisa*—which I had the chance to see when we lived in

Paris—but it was really hard to believe he was the same person who invented a machine whose sole purpose was to put gold sequins on women's dresses!

Anyway, none of us could come up with a really, really good plan to find the banner, and by the end of the day we were starting to feel a little discouraged. Tomorrow was a big day for Gia and Marco and the Torre. Tomorrow, the ten horses chosen to race in the Palio were to be announced. We could tell both of our friends were pretty anxious over the whole thing.

What if Scroscio were chosen, and she didn't have the banner back for the parade? We all wondered.

And what if Scroscio *wasn't* chosen for this Palio?

Gia and Marco would be crushed!

That's when I decided we needed another crack at Antonio. We needed to visit the café once again and have another look around.

As honorary Torre members, we felt we owed it to the contrada to do whatever we could!

Before Gia and Marco left for the evening, they cooked us an incredible dinner back at the residenza. Fresh pasta with homemade tomato sauce, and Italian bread. It was *so* yummy! We all laughed as Miss O followed them around the kitchen as they cooked, taking notes on everything they did.

"I want to make this exact same thing for my parents when I get back home," she told us. "I want it to come out just like this, too!"

We ate our dinner on the terrazzo, and talked about how pretty Siena was at night. We really had the best view. The lights along the Piazza del Campo were shining, and the *luna* (moon) lit up the night sky. In the background you could just make out the shadows of the Tuscan mountains. It was as pretty as a postcard! I took some pictures, setting the shutter speed really, really slow, and I crossed my fingers and prayed they would come out.

When my father walked through the door, he was excited to find a home-cooked dinner waiting for him. We sat with him as he ate and told him all about the crazy morning we'd had at the Tartuca museum and how we nearly got caught spying. And we told him about the Leonardo da Vinci museum and the wacky inventions the artist had spent years illustrating.

"We should bring your mother there when she comes," he suggested.

I nodded. "That would be great. She'll love it." Plus, I added—to myself only —with the three of us visiting a museum together, it will be just like old times back when we lived in Paris! That would be fun.

We waited for him to finish eating, then begged him to come down to the café with us for another night of spying. He said he had a few things to finish up on his laptop, so it all worked out as he joined us at the café again, sitting a table or two away from us.

Antonio noticed us when we got there, but I could tell he was trying not to look in our direction. He was avoiding us! He even sent another waiter over to our table to take our order.

We sat there for a while, nibbling on our gelatos, doing our best to find something—anything—out of the ordinary. But there was nothing. Nothing we could understand anyway! No talk about the Palio, no mention of the Tartuca . . . nothing. It was strange to think that the most important event in all of Siena would be taking place in just a few days, steps away from where we were sitting.

"This is silly!" Harlie finally said. "Nothing is happening!"

"I know," Miss O said in agreement. "How much longer do we have to sit here?" she asked me.

I felt a little responsible because, after all, it had been my idea to come down to the café to spy. Now that we were here, and things were oddly quiet, I realized it wasn't such a great idea after all. There was absolutely nothing going on!

"Okay," I said glumly. "I guess we can call it a night. But first, let's see if Antonio is still talking to us."

The girls watched as I caught Antonio's attention and waved him over. Reluctantly, he approached the table.

"Si?" he asked in a pretty unfriendly manner.

"Hi, Antonio," I said. "I was just wondering. Why is it so quiet here tonight?"

"Tomorrow is a very big day," Antonio replied. "Everybody is anxious. Nervous. Tomorrow the horses are chosen for the Palio."

"But tell me, Signorina Justine ," he began.

I gazed up at him. "Tell you what?" I asked.

"Are you and your friends spying on me for the Torre?"

I swallowed hard. "Uh, no! Uh-uh. We're not!" I stuttered.

The girls all shook their heads in agreement.

"Us?" Harlie asked. "Spies? No way! We're just kids!"

Antonio made a face. "I see you with the Torre in the car," he said. "So I think, you must be with the Torre."

"Gia is just our tour guide," I told him. "My father works during the day, and she is watching us and taking us sightseeing," I added. "Right, Dad?" I called to him at the next table.

Dad waved to us. "Right!" he said. "You must be Antonio," he said. "I am Justine's father. It's nice to meet you. The girls all love your gelato," he added.

"And your biscotti!" Harlie piped in.

My father went back to his laptop, and Antonio finally seemed convinced. I was so relieved! What kind of spies would we be if we got caught on our first day of spying?

"I think we should get going," I told the girls. "We have a big day tomorrow," I added. "We are going to Florence," I added, loud enough for Antonio to hear. I didn't really know if that was true, but I wanted to back up my "we're just touring and sightseeing" story.

"Firenze, —that's Florence in Italian—it is very beautiful," Antonio told us. "You will have a nice time there. I will be here tomorrow to learn of the horses' selection. Will you come to the café tomorrow?"

I nodded. "Yup!" I said. "For sure! How do you say, 'good luck' in Italian?" I asked him.

Antonio smiled. "*Buona fortuna*," he replied.

"Then buona fortuna!" I said.

"Grazie, Justine . Grazie. See you tomorrow."

Once upstairs, we all breathed a sigh of relief.

"I think we convinced him!" Miss O said, falling onto the sofa. "But boy-oh-boy, this spying stuff is hard work!"

"Tell me about it!" Juliette replied, taking a seat on the sofa next to her sister.

"I feel sort of bad lying to Antonio," I commented, sitting across from them. "But then I remind myself that he is against Gia and Marco," I added. "And he stole their banner! So then I don't feel so bad!"

"Right!" Harlie agreed. "Antonio is Tartuca! The enemy!" she said.

I let out a laugh. "Can you believe we are involved in this whole thing?" I asked my friends. "A big scandal in Siena! And we're caught in the middle of it all!"

"I think it's cool," Isabella agreed. "It would be even cooler if we could find the banner and return it to the Torre before the big parade."

"Yeah, I really want to find that banner," Juliette added. "And I want to write a story about the whole thing, too. A mystery!"

"That would be great, Juliette!" I said. "Would we all be in it?"

"Of course!" she replied. "You'll all be the main characters!"

I knew Juliette would write an awesome story about our adventures in Italy. She is a great writer. She always gets A's on all her reports and stuff at school, and once she won a writing contest at Sage.

I suddenly thought about home and how much I missed my mom.

"I'm gonna send an e-mail back home," I told the girls.

"Oooh! Good idea!" Miss O said. "We'll write home, too!"

"Me, too!" Harlie chimed in. "I want to see how my mom is feeling. I really miss her."

"Do you think she had the baby yet?" Miss O asked.

Harlie shook her head. "No way, she would have called me. I made her promise! And she isn't due to have the baby for another two weeks. After I get home."

I thought that when Harlie spoke about her mother, she sounded kind of homesick. She must have been putting up a good front so we couldn't tell. I know a lot about homesickness—from having traveled around so much with my parents. I suddenly had an idea that might help her.

I found Dad's laptop and logged onto my e-mail server. Then I attached my digital camera to the laptop and downloaded the pictures I'd taken so far.

"Let's send our parents e-postcards!" I said to the girls. "It'll be fun! We can write messages and captions to go with the pictures, too."

Harlie's eyes lit up. "Cool!" she said. "And can I check to see if my father is online?" she asked. "Maybe I can chat with him."

"Definitely," I told her. I logged onto my buddy list for Harlie and put in her father's screen name. Sure enough, Harlie's dad was online! It was seven hours earlier back home, so Harlie clicked on his name to chat. Her face brightened as she spoke with him, typing fast and furiously.

When she was finished, I wrote a long e-mail to my mother, telling her about all the excitement going on here in Italy. I attached a few pictures, too, then I hit SEND and passed the laptop to Miss O and Juliette. They logged onto their buddy lists and found their mother online! We all chatted with her for a while (Juliette even used some new Italian words we'd learned), then it was Isabella's turn. Her parents weren't online, but she sent them an e-postcard.

Before logging off, I decided to do a little research on the Web about the Palio. Boy was I surprised when I found pages and pages of articles and information about it!

"Listen to this!" I announced to the girls. "This article is about the contrade and how they take the Palio competition as far as to lie, cheat, and *steal* just to win!"

"Just like the Tartuca!" Juliette pointed out.

"And it says it's been this way for hundreds of years," I read on. "Some families forbid their children to play with children from other contrade. And even if two people from different neighborhoods meet and fall in love, their families won't let them marry out of the contrada!"

"That's crazy!" Isabella commented.

"Look! Here are some pictures from the Palio last summer," I said.

The girls crowded around the laptop. We gazed at the photos, which were taken at the Piazza del Campo right downstairs. You could barely see the cobblestone street, it was so mobbed. People waved flags and cheered in the pictures. It was a real scene.

"So many people!" Miss O remarked. "It really *is* a big deal!"

"That's what it's going to be like in three days from now?" Harlie asked.

I nodded. "I think so," I said. "It looks so colorful and festive," I added.

"Should we make posters?" Miss O asked. "You know, that say, 'Go, Scroscio!'"

I nodded eagerly. "Yes! We definitely should! We can hang them from the terrazzo. That would be way cool!"

"And let's decorate T-shirts!" Isabella added. "I have fabric markers with me."

"You do?" I asked.

Isabella nodded. "Yup. I always bring them on vacation and to horseback-riding camp. It's so people can sign my T-shirt on the last day. It makes a great souvenir."

"That's a good idea," I told her.

"Let's get started then," Miss O decided. "I'll find something we can use to make signs, and Isabella can get her fabric pens."

"Ooh! You know those white T-shirts we bought on the first day? The ones that say, 'SIENA' on the front? We should decorate those!" Juliette suggested.

"Yes! Let's do that!" Harlie agreed.

So it was all set. We were ready to turn our residenza into Palio central. We were going to make it look like the biggest Scroscio fan club in all of Italy!

The following morning, Gia and Marco came to the residenza to get us. It was actually true—we were going to Florence for the day! So I hadn't lied to Antonio after all.

They both wanted to get an early start, in order to get back in time to hear the big announcement and find out whether Scroscio had made the cut and would be racing in the Palio.

We piled into the minivan and headed for the city of Florence. Gia explained that we couldn't possibly see all of Florence in just one day, so we would only be visiting the city center, then going to Florence's version of New York City's Central Park.

"Bring your bathing suits!" Gia told us. "There is a wonderful swimming pool in the park—I thought we could have a picnic there and go for a swim."

Excitedly, we packed our suits in daypacks, grabbed a water bottle and followed Gia and Marco to the minivan downstairs. It was hot outside, so we were especially glad to hear we'd be swimming!

We spent the morning (before it got *too* hot) walking through the city streets of Florence, which Gia explained was a medieval city. There were so many art museums in Florence, it seemed that every building was either a museum or an art gallery! On the streets, many artists had set up their easels and paints and were painting landscapes of Florence.

"I would love to do that!" Miss O gushed as we went from artist to artist looking to see what they were making. Along with baking and soccer, Miss O had a passion for art, and she was very good at it. I love art, too, but I'm much better at sculpture and making jewelry. In fact, today I was wearing the coolest pair of earrings that I had made out of painted glass beads. One artist even asked me where I had got them! She was totally impressed when I'd told her I'd made them myself.

"Oooh, look! A gelato place!" Harlie cried as we stepped onto a street crammed with restaurants and outdoor cafés.

"It's only ten o'clock in the morning, Harlie," I pointed out.

"So?" Harlie demanded.

I shrugged. "I guess you're right. There's no *bad* time to eat gelato!"

So we stopped at a pretty café for some breakfast gelato—I tried the mango gelato, and Harlie got blueberry again. ("I really like this flavor," she said.) Isabella tried banana gelato, and Miss O and Juliette shared something chocolaty.

The Parco delle Cascine was awesome—just like Gia had said it would be. Harlie said it reminded her of Central Park, but that the swimming pool here was much nicer. We swam for an hour, which was great because it had turned really, really hot outside!

In the pool, Marco taught us the "Italian" way to play "Marco Polo," which wasn't so different from the way we play it in the United States. The funny thing was, every time one of us called, "Marco!" Marco would call back, "Sì? What do you want?"

We were drying off when Gia's cell phone rang.

"It is Papà!" she told us, looking at the caller ID. She flipped open the cell, and we sat in silence, waiting breathlessly to hear the news.

Gia's expression gave her away immediately. She smiled from ear to ear, then announced to us all, "Scroscio will race in the Palio!" she cried.

Marco cheered and did a backward flip into the pool. We all followed him in and celebrated the news splashing and cheering like crazy!

Mappa

Library

Great Hall

Hall

Gallery

Tartuca Museum

Chapter 9

Mission: Impossible!

Back at the estate that evening, the Reganato's main house was in full party mode! Gia's father had invited practically the entire contrada over to celebrate. There was more food than I had ever seen in one place before, and the adults were drinking a wine called Chianti. The crazy thing was, they were drinking the wine out of baby bottles! Gia explained that was because Palio time was like a "rebirth," so everybody honored Siena by drinking from bottles. It was so funny to see Papa Reganato drinking from a baby bottle!

My father met us at the estate and he joined in the celebration, too.

(We all cracked up watching him drink a baby bottle full of wine! It was even funnier because he was wearing his general's uniform!) It was really one of the best nights in Italy so far, I thought. I couldn't even imagine how amazing it would be if Scroscio did indeed win the race this weekend. The Torre would probably celebrate like July 4th or something. I really hoped that would happen.

We were stuffing our faces with pasta—all kinds of pasta!—when Gia came over to our table and asked us if we had seen Marco.

"Mmm," I tried to say, just having put a forkful of ravioli in my mouth. I shook my head, then swallowed. "No," I told her.

"I don't see him anywhere," Gia said. "If you see him, please tell him I am looking for him. Okay?"

"Sure," I replied. When she left, I suggested that we look for Marco ourselves.

We got rid of our plates, then roamed through the main house, searching for Marco. But Gia was right—he wasn't anywhere to be found. That was strange, I thought. He should be here celebrating with everyone else.

Harlie suggested we take a look outside. We followed her out the front door, then over to the guest house. As we walked, Juliette noticed a light on in the stables.

"Maybe he is with Scroscio?" Isabella suggested. "Let's go see. I'd like to see Scroscio anyway! And wish her buona fortuna!"

"Me, too!" I said. "Come on!"

We headed along the path from the guest house, past the carriage house and toward the stables. As we approached the entrance, we could hear hushed voices coming from inside.

"Shh!" I said to the others. "Someone is in there!"

We tiptoed quietly up to the entrance, then stepped inside.

On the floor of the stables sat Marco, surrounded by five other boys. They were huddled over a piece of paper, whispering furiously. Something serious was definitely going on. When they noticed us, they all stopped talking at once.

"What's going on, Marco?" I asked.

One of the other boys spoke harshly in Italian to Marco. We didn't understand what he was saying at all.

"It's okay!" Marco told his friends. "They are friends of the Torre. They are *my* friends."

One of the other boys opened his mouth in protest, but Marco shook his head. "It is okay to tell them," he assured him. "They want to help us!"

"What are you doing?" I asked.

Marco passed me the paper he had been looking at with his friends. It was a drawing of some sort—a map, maybe?

"What's this?" I asked.

"It is a map of the Tartuca museum," Marco explained. "We are going to go there tonight," he added. "And steal back our banner!"

I suddenly felt a little nauseated. I mean, they were planning something dangerous—all because we told him we *thought* the banner might be at the museum!

"Um, are you sure, Marco?" I asked.

"That sounds dangerous," Miss O added. "What if you get caught?"

Marco waved her off. "We will not get caught," he assured us.

But how could he know that? I wondered. I mean, what if they *did* get caught? They might get hurt or something. I thought about that article I'd read on the Internet about the Palio and the dirty tricks the contrade sink to in order to get revenge or whatever. If anything happened to Marco and his friends, it would be partly our fault!

"Can't you get the police to go there instead?" I asked.

Marco shook his head. "No! This is something I must do myself. Me and my friends."

"But if you *do* get caught," Harlie said, "what if Scroscio gets cut from the race? That would be terrible!"

"It is more terrible that the Tartuca have stolen our prized possession," Marco explained. "It is indeed wonderful that Scroscio has been selected for the Palio. But it will be a tragedy if she cannot march in the parade with our banner!"

"But what if I was wrong?" I asked him. "What if the banner is not there? We never actually saw what was in that sack," I reminded him.

"We have to take this chance," Marco replied. "It is very important to the Torre that we get our banner back. Almost as important as winning the Palio!"

There was nothing I could say or do to change Marco's mind. He was dead set on this recovery mission! All I could do was pray that he and his friends wouldn't get caught.

"I understand," I said finally. "We came out here to wish Scroscio buona fortuna, but I think you and your friends need it more!"

"Buona fortuna, Marco," I said anxiously.

"Buonoa fortuna," the girls echoed.

Marco smiled. "Grazie," he replied.

A while later we took a taxi back to the residenza, but before we entered the building, we noticed a commotion on the piazza. We walked to the corner and stood outside the café.

Harlie spotted the parade first, moving toward us along the Piazza del Campo. We could hear loud music and cheering—it sounded as if a parade of celebrities were approaching! I grabbed my digital camera and started to take pictures. As the parade came closer, we could see the flags the marchers were waving through the air.

They were the flags of the Tartuca!

"There's Antonio!" Miss O shouted above the noise.

"He's waving a Tartuca flag!" Isabella pointed out. "I bet you they have a horse that was chosen, too!"

I nodded and continued snapping away. The noise grew even louder as the parade passed the café—everyone was screaming and cheering, and a few pounded drums and rang bells.

"Look! That must be their horse!" Juliette cried, pointing to a beautiful white horse in the middle of it all. "Look at her cloak! It's so pretty!"

I took a picture of the horse, marching proudly along the piazza, a multicolored cloak with the Tartuca emblem of a tortoise on her back. She looked amazing—almost magical!

Antonio spotted us and left the parade to say hello.

"Our horse from the Tartuca has been chosen to race!" he cried excitedly. "Her name is *Allegra!*"

"Yes! We can see that!" I shouted to him. "She is a beautiful horse!" I added.

A crowd of people suddenly swarmed around Antonio and began hugging him and cheering. We took a few steps back, toward where my father was waiting, in order not to be stampeded by the mob.

"Allegra will win the Palio!" Antonio called out to us as the crowd lifted him up and carried him back to the parade. "The Torre will never win!" he added loudly. "Not without their good luck charm!"

Then suddenly Antonio was gone, back among the celebrating Tartuca marchers. The girls and I stood at the corner and watched, with our jaws hanging open

"Did you hear that?" Miss O asked me.

I nodded in horror.

"There's no question about it now," Isabella cried. "Antonio definitely stole the Torre banner!"

It was true. Antonio had been all too confident about Allegra winning the race. And he knew all about the banner having been taken.

He *had* to have taken it!

We turned back toward the residenza and headed upstairs for the night.

I closed my eyes and silently hoped that Marco's secret "mission impossible" was, at that very moment, going successfully.

Chapter 10
My Picture Is Worth
a Thousand Words

The next morning, none of us heard the alarm clock. We were all dead
tired! Maybe it was because we had stayed up so late the night before,
worrying about Marco.

My father came in at 9:00 to wake us up. I bolted up in bed and
asked him immediately.

"Did you hear from Marco yet?"

My father shook his head. "No, honey. Not yet."

I sighed, then fell back on my pillow.

"Do you think they stole back the banner?" Harlie asked from her sofa bed.

"I hope so," I replied.

"This waiting is killing me!" Miss O cried as she got out of bed. "I hope Gia and Marco come for us soon. I just have to know if they found that banner!"

"Me, too," I said, getting out of bed. "Let's get dressed so we'll be ready when they get here," I suggested.

We all got out of bed and got dressed. Nobody said a word! All we could think about was Marco and the banner. What if he hadn't found it at the museum? I wondered. Where, then, could it be? Marco and Gia and all their family and friends would be so disappointed if they couldn't recover the banner in time for Scroscio's parade.

We were having breakfast when we heard Gia's knock on the door. I bolted up from my chair and raced to the door. The girls all followed close behind me. When I flung open the door, I could tell by the expression on Marco's face that he had been unsuccessful.

"No!" I cried.

Marco hung his head. "We could not find it," he said glumly.

"I'm so sorry, Marco!" I said. "I wish there was something I could do!"

The girls offered their condolences, too.

"But you have to be happy!" Isabella urged him. "Scroscio is running in the Palio! That is amazing!"

Marco nodded. "I know," he said. "But without the banner, it will not be the same."

Just then, my father came to the door, ready to leave for work. "I'm sorry to hear about the banner," he said to Marco. "We were all hoping it would be recovered by now."

"Grazie, signore," Marco replied.

"Well, I know it isn't the banner," my father went on, "but I *do* have something I think will cheer you up!"

We all looked up at my father.

"What is it, Dad?" I asked.

He then reached into his briefcase and pulled out what looked like a bunch of cards. Marco's face lit up instantly.

"I know what this is!" he cried. "Wow! Grazie! Grazie mille! Thank you so much!"

"What is it, Marco?" I asked, trying to steal a peek at the cards.

"These are tickets to A.C. Siena!" Marco reported. "For today!"

"A.C. Siena?" Harlie asked. "What is that?"

"Duh!" Miss O declared. "It's a soccer team! Those are tickets to an A.C. Siena game!" She pulled them away from Marco and danced around excitedly as she read the tickets. "And they are playing A.C. Milan!" she cried. "How cool is that?"

"Mille cool!" Marco agreed.

We laughed. It was nice to see Marco all happy again. And though I don't particularly love soccer—nowhere near as much Miss O does, anyway—it would be fun to go to a professional Italian soccer game.

"There are enough tickets for everyone," my father told us before he left. "I wish I could join you, but I'm really swamped at the office today. Have fun!"

The mood was lifted as we got into the minivan and headed for the soccer stadium. I was so grateful to my father for helping to cheer up Marco and Gia. He was being such an awesome dad!

In the van, Marco explained to us some of the rules of soccer. With some help from Miss O, that is. He told us all about penalties and yellow cards—and the dreaded red cards, which meant that a player was out of the game. But the most exciting part of an Italian game, Marco told us, are the fans.

"They are *pazzo*!" Marco told us.

"What does that mean?" Harlie asked.

"*Loco!* " Isabella said in Spanish.

"*Fou!* " I chimed in French.

"Crazy!" Gia explained in English. "Italian soccer fans are the craziest fans in the world!"

She wasn't lying about that either. As we sat in the stands and cheered for A.C. Siena, we were blown away by the excitement of the spectators. It was wild! People were singing and cheering and screaming all throughout the game! Some people had their faces painted in their favorite team's colors, and many of them waved team pennants. A few of them wore woolen scarves, too, which was nuts because it was so hot.

The game was a lot of fun, and we were happy that A.C. Siena beat A.C. Milan 2–1. Marco was still happy and excited on the ride home, singing in Italian one of the cheers we had heard at the game.

"You think this was crazy?" he asked us. "Just wait until the Palio! The crowd there makes the soccer crowd look like they're sleeping!"

Wow. That was going to be something!

I sat back in my seat as we drove back to the place we were going for dinner. Gia was taking us to a small restaurant in Siena where you get to make your own pizza! You get dough and fresh mozzarella cheese and you can pick from a list of toppings. We were all pretty excited (and hungry). As the girls talked about what toppings they were going to put on their pizzas, I pulled out my digital camera to take a look at some of the pictures I had taken so far.

I scrolled through the pictures from Florence I had taken yesterday, then through the pictures I had snapped at the estate at the celebration last night. Then I came to the pictures from the piazza last night—of the Tartuca parade.

I had managed to take a really nice picture of Allegra, but I didn't dare show that to Marco. I quickly flipped to the next photo, when something caught my eye.

It was a picture of Antonio, marching in the parade, right before he joined us on the corner. I hit the zoom button and zoomed in closer. Then closer.

And that's when I noticed it.

In the picture, Antonio was holding the burlap sack!

At first, I didn't plan on showing Marco the picture. The last time I had told him about the sack, he'd gone and burglarized the Tartuca museum! There was no telling what he might do if he saw my picture of Antonio holding the sack.

Quietly, I nudged Harlie. She leaned over to me and peered at the digital camera screen. Her eyes widened as she realized what I was showing her.

"Holy cannoli!" she cried.

A little too loudly, I might add.

"What is it?" Miss O asked.

Everyone was staring at me, holding the camera.

"I . . . I . . . " I stuttered.

Harlie grabbed the camera from my hands. "Look at this!" she exclaimed. She thrust the camera into Marco's hands. "It's the sack!"

Marco's jaw fell open as he looked at the picture. "Is that the sack with the Torre banner?" he asked me.

"Um, well, it's the sack we saw at the museum the other day," I admitted. "But we never looked in it, Marco! We don't know for sure that the banner is in there!" I was all nervous again, with a sick feeling in my stomach. What was Marco going to do now, knowing that Antonio definitely had that sack?

Marco began shouting in Italian to Gia as she drove. I could tell they were arguing. Gia didn't seem to be agreeing with whatever Marco was saying. Finally, he sat back in his seat and flipped open his cell phone.

"We still have a chance at getting the banner back before the Parata del Palio tomorrow night!" Marco insisted as he dialed.

"But I don't think it is a good idea!" Gia told him.

"What does he want to do?" I asked.

Gia sighed as Marco began speaking to someone on his cell. "He wants to look for the banner tonight," she said. "He thinks maybe the Tartuca are hiding it in their Palio horse's stable."

"You mean he wants to break into Allegra's stable?" I asked in surprise.

"Sì," Gia replied.

"But . . . but why doesn't he just call the police?" I asked.

"You see what my brother is like!" Gia told us. "He is hot-headed! He feels he must do this himself. To bring honor back to the Torre and to our family."

"Oh, brother!" Harlie muttered.

"Sì!" Gia agreed. "Oh, *my* brother!"

That night, we ate dinner at the residenza with my father. Gia had dropped us off, then driven home with Marco, hoping to persuade him to change his mind and call the police. But I had the feeling she would not be able to get him to change his mind. Like Gia had said before, her brother was very hot-headed!

Dad noticed something was going on as we sat around the dinner table. I'm guessing it was because we weren't our usual, noisy selves, but to tell you the truth we were really nervous about Marco's new mission impossible. And we couldn't talk to my father about it because Marco had sworn us to secrecy!

"So a horse walks into a bar . . ." my father said suddenly.

"Huh?" I asked. We all looked up at him in confusion.

"It's a *joke*," he explained. "I'm trying to brighten the mood around here."

"Oh!" I said.

"So, a horse walks into a bar," my father said again. "And the bartender says to him, 'Why the long face?'"

Harlie giggled. "That's kind of funny," she said. "Get it?" she asked us. "Because all horses have long faces," she explained.

It *was* slightly funny, but I wasn't in a joking kind of mood.

"Funny, Dad," I said as I picked at my salad.

"What is with you girls this evening?" he then asked. "Is it my cooking? My jokes? Did you have a rotten time at the soccer game?"

Miss O perked up at the mention of the game. "Oh, no!" she said. "It was great! Awesome!"

"Yeah, it was really fun, Dad," I said. "The best! We're just a little bummed because of the whole banner thing," I added. "That's all."

"Yeah, it's the banner thing," Harlie agreed. "Because your dinner is great, and the joke was funny!"

"Thanks, Harlie," Dad said with a smile. "Glad you like them both! But I can only take credit for the joke. The dinner is actually from a restaurant down the block!"

"It's all excellent," Juliette chimed in. "And thanks again for the soccer tickets. We really had a great time."

"So how about some gelato to finish the evening with?" Dad suddenly suggested.

"Can we go to the café downstairs?" I asked quickly.

Dad shrugged. "Sure," he said. "If that's where you want to go. But I thought we would try another cafe—"

"No!" I insisted. "The one downstairs is fine. Thanks! We'll go get ready."

We cleaned up our plates and cleared the table. Then the girls followed me into the bedroom to wash up.

"How come you want to go to Antonio's café?" Isabella asked while we were getting ready.

"Well, I think I'll feel better if we can keep an eye on Antonio," I told her. "Especially tonight—while Marco is, you know, breaking into Allegra's stable."

"Good idea," Juliette said. "I'll feel better about the whole 'breaking and entering' thing, too, if we know where Antonio is at all times!"

Downstairs, the café was bustling as usual. In addition to the usual crowd of tourists and regulars, there were many people still celebrating Allegra's admission in the Palio. I figured they were all from the Tartuca, and I was a little relieved. At least if they were here at the café, they wouldn't be back at Allegra's stable!

We sat at our usual table and waited for Antonio to come take our gelato orders.

"Do you see him?" I asked the others. My heart was racing. What if he wasn't working tonight? I wondered nervously. What if he was at Allegra's stables tonight and he's there when Marco and his friends—

Before I could finish my horrible thought, Antonio appeared in front of me.

"*Buona sera, signorine!*" he said happily. "Good evening! Gelato?"

I sighed with relief. "Yeah, sure!" I said. "I'll have pineapple today," I told him.

"Strawberry for me," Miss O added.

"Coconut," Juliette said.

"And I think I'll try the lemon," Isabella ordered.

We all looked at Harlie.

"What?" she asked. "Blueberry. Duh!"

I laughed.

"Dad, aren't you having gelato tonight?" I asked.

"Of course!" he exclaimed. "Chocolate for me," he said to Antonio.

Antonio left to get our gelato, and we sat at the table gazing around the café.

"Okay, I give up!" my father said finally. "What is going on? You girls are way too quiet tonight! I know something is up!"

The girls all looked at me, and I knew I had to tell my father everything. Why? Because I can't lie to him. I never have, and I never will.

"Here's the thing, Dad," I began. "I saw something in one of my pictures today, on my digital camera screen, and it was something that made Marco want to do something stupid."

My father's eyes narrowed. "How so?" he asked.

"Well, I noticed in one of my pictures from the Tartuca parade last night that Antonio was carrying the sack. The same sack we think is hiding the stolen banner."

"The one Marco went looking for in the Tartuca museum?" he asked me.

I nodded. "Yes. Now he thinks the banner is being hidden in Allegra's stable," I said. "And tonight, he and his friends are sneaking in to steal it back."

I knew this news would upset my father, and I was right.

"Well, I'm grateful he didn't ask you girls to go with him," he said. "Because you can call it whatever you want—it is still breaking and entering. And stealing! Even if it *is* stealing back something that was first stolen," he added.

"I know, Dad," I said. "We feel terrible about this. So does Gia—she tried to talk her brother out of going, but he wouldn't listen to her."

Just then, Antonio arrived with our gelatos. I made a face at my father to let him know we shouldn't talk about this in front of Antonio. Dad caught on.

"So tomorrow," he said, changing the tone in his voice, "how about we go to Pisa?"

"For real?" I asked, wondering if he was just saying that to cover up what we'd been talking about.

"Absolutely!" he replied. "I can go into the office later in the day. It will be fun to go sightseeing with all of you!"

"There is a tower in Pisa," Antonio told us as he handed out spoons for the gelato.

We all cracked up.

"Duh!" Harlie said, digging into her blueberry.

Antonio laughed, too. "I was only making a joke," he said. "I know that everybody in the world knows about the Leaning Tower."

"So how about it, girls?" Dad asked. "Shall we go see this Leaning Tower for ourselves tomorrow?"

We all lit up and nodded.

"Definitely!" Miss O cried.

"Cool!" Juliette added.

"Do you need me to come with you, to point it out?" Antonio asked with a grin.

"Ha! No, thanks!" I said. "I'm sure we'll know which one is the leaning tower!"

Antonio was still chuckling as he walked away. As soon as he was out of sight, my father opened his cell.

"I'm calling Franco Reganato," he said. "I want him to know that his son might be in danger."

We all ate our gelato in silence as my father dialed. I knew I had done the right thing by telling him, but I felt really sick to my stomach. I hoped Marco would forgive me!

I listened as my father explained to Marco's father what I'd told him. All my father kept saying was "Oh!" and "I see." I couldn't imagine what Mr. Reganato was saying to him!

Finally, my dad snapped his cell shut. We all put down our spoons to hear what he had to say.

"I was too late," he explained. "Marco and his friends broke into Allegra's stable a little while ago."

I gasped. "And?" I asked in alarm.

"They found the sack," my father told us. "But it was empty."

Chapter 11
Leaning Torre . . . and Pisa

The next day, Dad rented a minivan for the day, and we headed to the city of Pisa. Now that we knew Marco was fine and that he and his friends had not been caught at Allegra's stable last night, we could all rest easier. It was a bummer, though, that they had not been able to recover the banner.

I was determined to enjoy Pisa though, and I tried to push all thoughts of stolen banners and horse races out of my mind! Today was the first day my father was hanging in Italy with us and I wanted it to be a blast!

As we neared the city, we could already see the famous Leaning Tower in the distance. But we pretended we didn't see it, which was so funny!

"I don't know where it could be!" my father joked. "The map says it's around here somewhere!"

Harlie pointed to a smaller tower, which was so obviously *not* the famous one, and she cried out, "I found it! There it is!"

"No, it's over there!" Juliette said with a laugh, pointing to a building with a sign that said, *Banco d'Italia*. (It was a bank.)

It was silly, but we all cracked up anyway.

When we arrived at the real tower, which was built as part of a cathedral more than 800 years ago, we parked the rental van and raced toward it. It was crazy! The thing really did *lean*. And it leaned a lot! I couldn't imagine how it hadn't toppled over in the past 800 years!

The best, for me, was taking pictures of the tower. We found a spot on the south side of the tower where it wasn't so crowded with tourists. The girls ran up to the tower and pretended to hold it up—and I got some great shots! In one, they are all making faces as if to say, "This tower is so heavy to hold up!" That one was going to come out great!

We took a tour up to the top of the tower and we counted the steps as we went up. (There were 293, in case you were wondering.) Eight floors later, we were at the top. From there, the view of the city was incredible—you could see for miles and miles!

Juliette pulled out her journal and began writing something, but she wouldn't let us see what it was. Finally, she pulled out a sheet of paper and showed us. It said:

WHAT A FOREIGN STONE PILE!

"I don't get it," Harlie said.

"It's an anagram!" Juliette announced. "My social studies teacher did anagrams for us last year—of famous places and landmarks. If you rearrange all the letters, you can spell: 'The Leaning Tower of Pisa'!"

"No way!" Miss O insisted. Then she checked it out to find her sister was right. "That's pretty cool," she commented.

"Wow! Look down there!" Isabella cried. "They have scooters! Now *that's* what I call pretty cool!"

"I wish we could rent scooters," Harlie said.

I turned to my father. "Dad? Can we?" I asked. "Can we rent scooters?"

We all held our breath waiting for him to answer.

He shrugged. "I don't see why not," he replied. "As long as you wear helmets."

We cheered, then raced down the 293 steps back to the ground. Luckily, the scooter rental place was nearby, and the minimum age to rent scooters was ten! We were in luck!

For the next hour, we scootered all around Pisa. What a blast! My father rented one, too, and though they didn't go very fast, we raced them anyway.

Miss O came in first, and we decided to name her scooter "Scroscio."

When Harlie announced, "*Ho fame*," we all agreed with her and decided it was time for lunch. So we picked a café and ate our lunch looking at the Leaning Tower in the background. While we ate, we talked about how much fun we were having on vacation!

"Even though I feel bad for Marco and Gia," I told the girls, "it's still the most exciting vacation ever!"

They all agreed with me. Even my father said he was having a great time!

"I only wish we could help the Torre find their banner," Juliette said as she munched. "If only it were as easy as solving an anagram!"

"What I think you girls need," my father told us, "is a good army-style plan of action if you want to recover the stolen banner."

"Like what?" Harlie asked.

"Well, first you need a commander," he explained. "Someone chosen to make the decisions and execute the orders."

"Justine! You can be the commander!" Miss O exclaimed. "Maybe all that army stuff runs in the family!"

Oh, great, I thought. I'm so not the commander type.

"Next, you need a strong plan of action—especially for a mission of this nature," my dad went on. He used napkins and straws to map out his plan on the table. "For example, you may want to divide and conquer," he suggested, putting two straws near my glass of juice and two on the other end of the table near Isabella's fries. "Split up into two teams, A and B. One team can perform the night maneuvers and the other the day maneuvers."

Uh-oh, I thought to myself. *My father was being way too general-ish.*

"Now, the best way to approach a delicate reconnaissance mission is with a surprise attack." He covered the table with napkins, then looked up at us. "Are you following?" he asked.

"Sir, yes, sir!" Harlie exclaimed.

"Dad, is this really necessary?" I asked. "I mean, *night maneuvers*? We're only ten! How can we do night maneuvers when we have to be in bed at ten o'clock?"

I think my father suddenly realized he had gotten a little carried away. He smiled as he crumpled up the napkins and tossed them in the trash.

"You're right, Justine," he said sheepishly. "Just kidding."

"Thanks anyway, Dad," I said. "But I think we're better off staying out of all the Palio drama . . . and just following the race as tourists!"

"That's a good idea," he replied. "Now, it's after two o'clock and we still haven't had gelato today! That, my friends, is a true crime!"

That evening, we showered and wore our pajamas down to the piazza to watch Scroscio in her Parata del Palio. We were really excited about the festivities—I had *both* my cameras with me for the event! Unfortunately, we found the mood downstairs a bit glum. Way too glum for a contrada with a horse in the Palio, I thought.

But Marco had been right. Despite the fact that Scroscio would be racing in the Palio tomorrow, the contrada della Torre was having trouble celebrating in light of the stolen banner. There were some cheers and shouts as the beautiful, strong horse paraded around the piazza, but you could tell there was an underlying sadness.

So we tried to cheer everyone up!

We practiced our cheers—the Italian songs we had learned at the soccer game—and we wore our decorated SIENA T-shirts over our pajamas. Harlie—who is so good at gymnastics that she competes in meets all over New York—did some flips and handsprings while we sang and cheered on Scroscio.

All I could think about was how sad it was that Scroscio's parade was so lame, while Allegra's parade the other night was a spectacle! Didn't Scroscio deserve a better parade? I wondered.

When Marco marched by with Scroscio, we yelled and screamed as loud as we could. He really seemed grateful, too, as he waved back to us. Before we knew it, he was running toward us, waving at us frantically.

"Come join the parade!" he shouted to us. "Please! You are such devoted members of the Torre! We would be honored!"

The girls and I exchanged looks, then I shot a glance at my father.

"Dad?" I asked.

"Sure! Of course! Go ahead!" he called out. "Just stay with Gia and Marco!"

"Wait!" Isabella cried, just as we started to follow Marco. "We're in our pajamas!" she reminded us.

I laughed. "So what?" I called back. "We have to support Scroscio!"

Giggling like crazy, the five of us joined the Torre parade. I know we must have looked way silly, marching alongside a horse around the Piazza del Campo in our pajamas. But I really didn't care! It was fun! And the best part was, when people saw us, they cheered even louder for Scroscio!

When the parade was over, we were still giddy with excitement. I took pictures of my friends outside in their pajamas, then we danced and sang all the way back to the residenza. We felt proud to be Torre!

Now if only Scroscio could rise to the occasion and win the Palio tomorrow! How awesome would that be? And if Marco could see that happen, he would realize that it isn't luck that helps you win . . . it's the pride and support of your friends!

Chapter 12
Win, Place, or Show Me the Money!

The next morning, we were awakened by ringing bells. *Loud* bells!

"Turn off the alarm!" Harlie pleaded. She pulled her pillow over her head and rocked back and forth in the bed. "Can't a girl get any sleep around here?"

I rubbed the sleep from my own eyes and let out a huge yawn. "That isn't the alarm, Harlie," I said.

Harlie sat up in bed. "No? What is it then?"

I sat up, too. "Beats me," I said with a shrug.

"It's coming from outside," Miss O said sleepily. "What time is it anyway?"

"It's eight-thirty," I told them all. "Come on. Let's see what's going on."

We stumbled out of the bedroom and walked through the living room to the terrazzo doors. I pushed them open and we stepped outside, into the morning sun. Unbelievably so, we were the last ones awake in Siena, apparently! The piazza below was already filled with people!

"Holy cannoli!" Harlie cried. "What's going on? What are all those people doing down there?"

As far as I could see, there were crowds of people lining the sidewalks along the piazza. The stone street of the piazza was roped off, and yellow sand was being poured onto the square.

"I think," I told my friends, "they are here for the Palio!"

"This early?" Harlie asked in amazement. "Wow!"

"Well at least we don't have to go down there and look for seats," Miss O commented. "We have the best seats in the house!"

It was true. From our terrazzo we could see everything. The whole piazza!

"Come on!" I cried. "Let's get out our decorations!"

We raced back into the bedroom and pulled the posters and banners we'd made to cheer on Scroscio. Because we didn't have any art supplies with us on vacation, we had to make do with what we could find in the residenza. We used the laptop and printer to print some of the signs, but the best decoration was the banner we'd made from an old sheet given to us by one of the residenza chambermaids. We'd painted across it in big, bold letters:

GO!!!! Scroscio! Vai!
(Go!!!! Scroscio! Go!)

Miss O had painted a horse on one end of the banner, and then a crown on the other end.

Working together, we decked out the terrazzo until it looked like a Scroscio shrine! We hung shiny beads off the terrazzo posts (I had brought them along to wear with an outfit, but decided they worked much better as decorations) and we cut up buckets full of colored confetti—hopefully to toss off the terrazzo when Scroscio crossed the finish line first.

Decked out in our SIENA T-shirts, we each found a cozy waiting spot on the terrazzo. We would be spending the entire day there, since the race wasn't until later in the afternoon. We grabbed some yogurts and fruit and had breakfast out there, too. There was a celebration happening right on our doorstep, and we didn't want to miss a thing!

We sat there all afternoon, watching everything that went on, shouting down to the people below us and waving and cheering. Around noon, Gia, Marco, and their father surprised us by coming over to watch the race with us. We couldn't have been more excited. Papa Reganato cracked us up when he handed us flashing pacifiers—one for each of us.

He explained that the pacifiers are a symbol of the tenderness felt for the Palio banner, also known in Siena as *cittino*, or baby.

All throughout the afternoon, Papa Reganato, Marco, and Gia explained to us everything that was happening on the square below. We were so lucky to have them watch with us!

"You don't root for a particular jockey," Papa Reganato warned us. "Not in the Palio. All the jockeys are looked upon as traitors! They ride for the contrada that pays them the most money, and they can change horses any time they wish!"

"Really?" I asked. "That doesn't seem fair," I commented.

"Nothing about the Palio is fair!" Marco retorted.

"You see all the different flags?" Papa Reganato asked.

We nodded.

"Each crowd below sits with its own contrada," he explained. "You can tell the different contrade by their flag. Over there, that is the Torre."

We looked across the square to see the familiar elephant and tower emblem.

"Next to the Torre are the Snail, the Porcupine, the Unicorn, and the Shell. Over there," he went on, "you have the Caterpillar and the Panther. On that side is the Dragon, the Giraffe, the Eagle, the Forest, the Goose, and the Owl. And down below is the Wave, the She-Wolf, and the Tortoise."

"We know the Tortoise," Harlie pointed out. "Unfortunately," she added.

Papa Reganato chuckled. "I can see you have really gotten into the spirit of the Palio!" he said.

"We're rooting for Scroscio!" Miss O told him. "We are part of the Torre —Gia said so!"

"Yes, that is right," Papa Reganato replied. "Gia told me she made you honorary Torres. We are honored!"

I beamed. Coming from Franco Reganato—that was truly something special!

"Where are the horses going now?" Juliette asked, as we could see the horses being led away from the Piazza.

"Now they go to the church," Papa Reganato explained. "It is very special, this event. In the church, the horses are given the blessing for buona fortuna. Do you know what that is?"

"Good Luck!" we all cried.

"Sì. For good luck. Then they are told by the priests, 'Vai e torna vincitore! Go and return a winner!' In a little while, they will come back out to the piazza, and there will be a mad rush to find a seat near the finish line!"

"But aren't you supposed to sit with your contrada?" I asked.

Papa Reganato grinned at me. "Yes, you are!" he said. "But after the blessings, nobody really plays by the rules anymore. It gets out of control . . . it gets . . . "

"Pazzo!" I cried, remembering the Italian word for 'crazy' from the other day.

"You said it, Justine!" Marco told me with a wink.

We all stood, overlooking the Piazza, as the commotion grew to a frenzy. It was way crazier than the soccer game—that was for sure. But it was a lot like the game, too. The spectators down below waved flags, pennants and even wore scarves, despite the heat.

Before we knew it, it was 5:00 p.m. The official festivities were about to start. I glanced back down at the crowd, and aside from the yellow sand along the "racetrack" it looked like a sea of people! There wasn't an inch to budge!

Isabella pointed out the balconies and terraces all around the square . . . every single one was packed with people.

First came the parade. In contrast to the parades from the nights before, this parade was much slower and quieter. Each contrada paraded into the square wearing colorful costumes and waving silk banners with their emblems. They pushed carts and rode floats in a long line, one contrada after the other. At the very end of the parade, kind of like Santa at the Macy's Thanksgiving Day Parade, came the Palio victory wagon. It was pulled by four white oxen. On the wagon were two flags: the black-and-white flag of Siena, and the palio that the winning horse would soon win.

"That's the palio!" I cried. "Wow! It's so pretty!"

"Every year artists from all over Siena compete to design the palio," Gia explained. "It is a work of art!"

Suddenly, there was silence. We were all so stunned by the silence, we looked to Papa Reganato for an explanation.

He whispered to us, "*There is complete silence until the horses' starting positions are announced.*"

"*Oh!*" I whispered back. I couldn't believe thousands of people could be so quiet.

Then, all of a sudden, there was a roar from the crowd as the positions were announced! It took us all by surprise.

"Scroscio has the third slot!" Marco announced.

"Is that good?" I asked.

He nodded. "Yes. The first few slots are the best."

We watched in amazement as nine of the ten horses positioned themselves between two ropes, maneuvered by their jockeys into the correct order. It looked so disorganized, I thought. Not like any horse race I'd ever seen before.

"The tenth horse stays back, in a place behind the other horses," Papa Reganato explained. "This is really an important part of the race. This is the jockey who will decide when the race starts. When he 'takes off,' the race has officially begun!"

"That's nuts!" Harlie exclaimed. "How come he gets to decide?"

Papa Reganato shrugged. "That's just how it has always been," he said. "It is how the race officially begins. The jockey waits until he notices his rival horse is distracted. That is the perfect time for him to begin!"

We watched as the horses waited between the ropes for the rear horse in the tenth position to start. It was really taking a long time.

"What's taking so long?" Isabella asked.

"Oh, this can take up to an hour!" Marco told us. "It is all part of the tenth jockey's strategy. He wants to catch all the other horses off guard and get a head start."

A minute later, the horses took off! The race had begun! It was funny because even though we were expecting it, after waiting so long, we didn't expect it when it happened.

"Is this it?" I asked Papa Reganato.

"This is it!" he cried.

The girls and I started jumping up and down, cheering for Scroscio. But before we knew it, the horses were all called back to the starting line!

"A false start," Gia explained. "They must begin again."

"*Sheesh!*" Miss O cried. "This could take all night!"

"Si," Gia replied.

I felt as though we were standing there for the longest time after that. The suspense was killing me! Finally, before I knew it, the horses took off again. And this time, there was no false start!

Papa Reganato got up from his chair and leaned over the terrazzo. "*Now* this is it!" he cried.

I held my breath as I watched the horses race. It was so exciting! Like nothing I'd ever seen before. And the crowd? Pandemonium was the only word I could find to describe it.

"Take pictures!" Marco instructed. "The race will be over in seconds!"

Yikes! I thought.

"It's only about seventy-three seconds long," Gia added as the horses ran past our terrazzo for the first of three times. "*Vai, Scroscio!*" she shouted. "*Vai, vai, vai!*"

Everyone shouted and screamed and I held up my camera. I'd decided to take digital pictures of the race today, since I could snap more quickly than with my 35-millimeter. From behind the lens I watched the race as I pushed the shutter button as many times as possible.

"Look!" Harlie cried out. "Scroscio and Allegra are neck and neck!"

As the horses rounded the square the third and last time, racing toward the finish line, we all found ourselves jumping up and down with excitement. My heart was beating so fast, I thought it would burst out of my chest! I screamed at the top of my lungs, *"Run, Scroscio! Run!"*

And just like that . . . it was over.

Chapter 13

A Photo Finish!

Again, there was a deafening silence as all of Siena waited to hear the results of the race. My heart was still thumping, and I could even *feel* my blood circulating, that's how excited I was!

"I think I got a picture of the horses crossing the finish line!" I said breathlessly.

"Awesome, Justine!" Miss O said. "Maybe you can have it blown up or something when you get home. How cool will that look hanging in your room?"

I nodded, setting my digital camera to "view" so I could see what I'd got. But before I could look, a voice boomed throughout the square. Everyone's eyes rested on the podium: the results were now in.

I was worried that we wouldn't understand the results as they were announced in Italian, but it wasn't hard to figure out who had won. We all heard "Scroscio" and "Torre," and it was clear that our horse had come in first place!

The five of us were beyond ecstatic. We hugged each other and high-fived, and we jumped up and down and cheered with happiness. But it was nothing like what was going on across the square in the contrada della Torre. From our terrazzo, we could see it all. Everybody was hugging and kissing and dancing and shouting. The entire square was celebrating. We could *feel* their excitement!

In a flash, we found ourselves down on the piazza with the Reganatos. Groups of Torre members crowded around us, hugging and kissing us, too. It was so funny—they didn't even know us, but since we were with Marco and his family, we were considered Torre!

Before we knew what was happening, long, long tables were being set up along the square.

"I think the whole contrada della Torre is having dinner on the piazza tonight!" Miss O remarked. We watched in amazement as platters of food and pitchers of Chianti wine appeared out of nowhere. Baskets of bread, bowls of pasta, vegetables, meats . . . where had it all come from? It didn't matter—if you were celebrating with the Torre, you could have whatever you wanted!

There were plenty of kids our age around, too. Almost every one of them had a flashing pacifier! We felt right at home, cheering and singing along with them.

We sat down at one long table with my father and filled up on fettucini and soft, warm, freshly baked bread. Everybody who walked by yelled to us, *"Congratulazioni!"* and we yelled back, *"Salute!"* which, Gia explained, means "Cheers!"

I was feeling like a true Italian—that was for sure. I couldn't imagine being in Italy during any other time of the year. How awful would it have been to have come to Italy one week later and to have missed all this?

Finally, I had a chance to scroll through my photos from the race.

"Isabella!" I cried, "You are going to love this photo of Scroscio! I'm going to make copies and blow them up for all of you!"

"Awesome!" Isabella replied. "Make lots of copies for me. I want every single picture to hang in my room!"

I laughed, picturing Isabella's room with three hundred pictures of Scroscio hanging all over the place. Then I stopped laughing. I took a closer look at the photo I'd taken of the horses crossing the finish line.

I zoomed in for a better look.

No, I wasn't zooming in to see which horse had crossed first—that was obvious. Scroscio had won by more than head.

What I was looking at was Allegra . . . and what was sticking out from under her pretty, multicolored cloak.

"Holy cannoli!" I cried.

Miss O jumped out of her chair and came around to my side of the table. "What's up, Justine? What do you see?"

I held the camera out for her and the others to see.

"Look what's under Allegra's cloak!" I cried out in disbelief.

"*I think that's the stolen banner!*"

It was way too crowded for me to start looking for Marco. There were still thousands of people parading through the piazza! All I could do was wait until he came back from all the congratulating that was going on.

Luckily, I didn't have to wait long.

"Marco!" Juliette shouted. "Over here!"

Marco spotted us at our table and made his way over.

"Is this not the best night of your life?" he asked excitedly.

"It *is!*" I told him.

"Yeah, it's totally, completely pazzo!" Harlie piped in.

"Ha! Sì, Signorina Harlie! It is pazzo! Molto pazzo!"

"That's not all," Miss O told him. "Justine has something she wants you to see!"

I stood up and held out my camera. "I took a picture of the finish line," I told him. "I thought you might like to see what the *losing* horse was wearing under her cloak."

Marco's eyes narrowed at me as he took the camera. He peered at the screen, and his eyes grew wide with shock.

"It is the Torre palio!" he cried. "You found it!"

I was beaming with pride. "Yup!" I said nonchalantly.

"You are certainly the best photographer in the world!" Marco announced.

"Well, you know," I said casually. "I do what I can."

Marco gave me an enormous hug. Then he hugged Miss O, Harlie, Isabella, and Juliette, who couldn't hide her red face from being hugged by a crush.

"Grazie mille!" he said to us. "Thank you for finding our palio. I knew our Torre good luck charm had to be around here somewhere!"

"Well, I agree with you that the palio must be a good luck charm," I told him. "But I think it was more than luck that helped Scroscio win the race."

Marco nodded. "Sì," he said. "Scroscio won the race because of our new honorary Torre members who rooted for her!"

We all laughed.

It wasn't exactly what I had had in mind, but saying that I and my BFFs had helped win the Palio? I wasn't going to argue with *that*!

"Tell me, Signorina Justine," Marco said.

"Sì, Marco?"

"Will you still be in Italy on August sixteenth?" he asked.

"Um, well, yes, I will," I replied. "My friends will be back home in New York, but I will still be here in Siena."

"Oh! That is certainly *buone notizie!*" he exclaimed. "Good, good news for the Torre!"

"Good news for the Torre?" I asked in confusion. "How come?"

Marco smiled and a dark, black curl fell across his face. "Because on August sixteenth," he said, "we have the second Palio race of the summer!"